# OCCURRENCE AT LATIGO

## JACK R. STANLEY

Wrightbridge Press

# DEDICATION

*To the love of my life*
*Mary Lee*
*who makes all things possible.*

# TWO FREE E-BOOKS

*{Murder in Muleshoe}*
**If you were murdered would they try to find the killer or plan him a parade?**

*{Guns Along The Rio}Rio*
**In 1858, two fresh-off-the-ranch 17-year-olds join the Texas Rangers.  What could possibly go wrong?**

Click HERE to get your free books.

# CHAPTER 1

Five rough looking riders approached a bluff in broken country. This was mostly prairie. There were a few trees and stands of boulders. High up in the rocks a western rattlesnake coiled itself back into a defensive circle. A large man's boot was nearby but motionless at that moment. The man, almost a mountain unto himself, covered by a buffalo robe, had worked his way up behind a large boulder overlooking the on-coming riders. This was Tarr Phillips. Sighting down on them with his Winchester, he froze at the sound of the snake's rattle. The venomous creature was coiled only inches away from him and ready to strike.

Phillips looked down on the serpent with irritation. In a lightening quick move, he pinned the snakes' head under his boot.

He turned back to the riders. The one in the lead rode a dun and had his sweat soaked hat with the brim flatten up again the crown. Phillips set his sights on the scruffy rider's head, knowing the bullet would drop on its path to its target over the distance. The big man in the rocks squeezed the trigger slowly until his weapon jerked in his hands.

The first rider was thrown from his saddle with the slug catching him in the center of his chest. The others instantly jumped from their saddles and sought cover behind their horses. They threw wild shots in the general direction of the bluff. But these were pistol rounds and none actually made the height and position of Phillips.

Phillips ducked out of sight and turned his attention to the snake wrapping itself around his boot. He calmly took the reptile by the head and looked into its threatening eyes. The rattler wrapped itself around his arm.

"You stupid critter," he said.

With a flick of his big arm, Phillips flung the snake away. Then he retraced his path back down the rocks to his horse. The reptile, which had landed in between some rocks, slithered away into the shadows.

Down below on the other side of the boulder,

the riders continued to shoot wildly. It was their leader, Gus Fry, who waved them off. Fry had a gut that over-topped his belt and he was as dirty as he was out of shape.

He had made it to cover behind a rusted iron colored rock. He peered out and studied the bluff they were approaching.

Unseen by Fry or this gang, Phillips returned his rifle to its scabbard and climbed into the saddle of his dapple gray. He rode on.

It would be a while before Fry and his men did the same.

❧

THUNDER RUMBLED NOT FAR AWAY. IT HAD rained recently and would again, soon. It was spring in the Texas Hill Country. A pair of good but not matched sorrels pulled a relatively new farm wagon. The ground was already near to being an ocean of mud and the animals had to struggle. Ahead was the one street town of Latigo.

A man and a woman were mounted atop the wagon seat. The man, in his early 30's, wore a poncho and a soaked hat. He had broad shoulders and was clean shaven. He drove the wagon with an attractive woman, five years younger and wrapped in a blanket beside him. This was Lyles and Sarah Quinn.

A group of men on the porch of the town's lone saloon watched the Quinn's arrival.

Luther Bobbs, a feisty ol' ranch hand of 40, sat on an empty keg, carving on a block of wood with his pocket knife, and spat into the street. Beside him stood Fenn Burch, 50's, an aproned barkeep with a soft belly. His blonde hair was thinning.

A 36 year-old cowboy with a splint on one leg, Dave Shambow, stood pissing into a puddle beside the saloon. He had a coffee cup in his free hand. His hair was long and greasy and his beard was scraggy with missing patches were no hair grew at all.

Shambow spoke as the wagon passed nodding his head in greeting, "Lovely day, ma'am."

Shambow was pleased with himself. Fenn, the barkeep, popped Shambow on the arm with his bar towel.

Sarah turned away in disgust. Quinn didn't see Shambow as he was focused on guiding the wagon on down the muddy street.

Quinn stopped at the depot/general store. He was a fit man and very agile. He climbed down and helped his wife to the boardwalk. She went in under the overhang and looked up at him.

Sarah, wringing out her long chestnut hair, said

to her husband, "If you say so much as one little word to me, Lyles Quinn, just one, that sounds like 'I told you so' — I'll kick you, so help me Hanna!"

Lyles couldn't help but grin. "I'm not saying a thing," he said suppressing a laugh on his blue eyed face.

But after another moment, they both burst into laughter as they embraced. They shared something very special. And the love between them was not difficult to see.

# CHAPTER 2

Back on the porch of the saloon, Fenn, Bobbs, and Shambow watched the Quinns. The lame cowboy buttoned up his pants as he said, "Dumb sod buster. Why in th' hell bring somethin' as nice as that out here?"

The barkeep said, "Careful, Shambow. She's his wife. Livin' t'gether is what married folk do."

Shambow shook his head, "Won't be but a couple a' years 'fore she's as used up and worthless as that ground he's pickin' at. I ain't sayin' I'd mind doin' some of th' usin'?"

The older ranch hand, Luther Bobbs looked up from where he sat carving and said, "Shambow, how can you stand t' eat with th' same hole you talk with?"

"What?" Shambow asked as if he'd said nothing they weren't all thinking.

"That mouth of yours is going to get you killed," Fenn said as he wiped his hands on his apron, shook his head and went inside his saloon.

The inside of the Elite Saloon revealed nothing like its name. The place was plain, drab and barely a functional saloon.

A young gunfighter, Willy Hyer, sat playing an endless game of solitaire. The kid wasn't old enough to shave. His attempt at a mustache was laughable. He wore his pistol low slung. His attempt at swagger was as threatening as his flat coal black eyes.

There was a stove in the center of the saloon. Two farmers sat near the stove. Ned Guthrie, a tired looking late 30's, always seemed to be angry at the world. He wore a threadbare jacket, torn jeans, and down-in-the-heel boots. Jess St. Clair, approaching 50, was a weather-beaten, stoop-shouldered man with a determined face half covered with a throat length beard.

The barkeep crossed by the farmers and said, "Quinn jest come in."

St. Clair, the older of the two farmers, stood and pulled on his wet boots which had been drying beside the stove. He reached for his coat. Guthrie stayed seated.

St. Clair asked, "Ned, you comin'?"

"Directly," Ned Guthrie said.

The other farmer indicated he hadn't finished his drink.

St. Clair walked out to the porch.

Fenn got behind the bar as Shambow limped in, giving a dirty look to both farmers before he crossed to the bar. He picked up his empty coffee cup and showed it to Fenn.

"Coffee's free," the barkeep said returning to the stove and reaching for his pot. "but I could run out almost any time now, Shambow."

St. Clair walked across the saloon turning up his collar and went outside.

Shambow held his empty coffee cup to Fenn.

Shambow said, "I'll buy some more bad whiskey — in a while."

Fenn poured Shambow a cup of coffee, "Bad is the onlyest kind I have."

"Okay, damnit, give me a glass of it."

Shambow tossed a coin on the bar.

Fenn sat up a glass for Shambow who held his nose and drank.

"Damn! This crap tastes like somethin' you just spit in, Fenn."

"For you, Shambow, I just might," Fenn said recorking the bottle. Shambow turned his back to the bar and picked up his coffee looking out the front doors. "One of these days I'd like t' grab me a hand full of that little gal."

The gunfighter looked up from his card game. Guthrie looked up at Shambow.

The sullen farmer said, "Who you talkin' about, Shambow?"

"That little gal your boy Quinn married. She is one fine lookin' piece a' woman."

The barkeep warned, "Shambow!"

"Shut up, Fenn. Even farmers know what happens 'tween a bull an' a heifer."

Guthrie examined his drink, gulped it down and stood. He noted Shambow's coffee cup in the lame cowpuncher's hands. Guthrie elbowed the hot contents onto Shambow's injured leg. Shambow yelped in pain.

As Guthrie strode toward the door, the young gunfighter stuck out a leg in the farmer's path.

"That's kind'a like back shootin', ain't it!" Hyer asked.

Guthrie realized what Hyer was saying. The farmer swallowed hard.

"Man's got no right t' talk that'a'way 'bout a good woman."

"As I understand it, she's a farmer's bitch."

Fenn leaned across the bar with a .12 gauge single barreled pump shotgun in his hands aimed directly at Hyer.

"Less you figure you're faster than double o buck, mister, don't even think about movin'."

"Say, friend, I don't like people wavin' guns in my direction.

Fenn said, "I ain't wavin'. I'm dead center of your gut."

Hyer took a breath but decided that's all the moving he was interested in doing.

To the farmer, Fenn said, "Get out of here, Guthrie!"

Guthrie stepped around Hyer's leg and left with a little quicker step than before.

To the kid, Fenn said, "If you want t' stay in my place, drink my bad whiskey, an keep on breathin', you get back t' your card game."

"I learned a long time ago not to cross the barkeep."

Hyer slid back under the table and picked up the deck of cards.

Fenn slowly lowered his shotgun and returned it to its place under the bar. He picked up a new bottle and crossed to Hyer's table where he poured the gunfighter a drink.

"On th' house." Fenn said.

# CHAPTER 3

Over in the freight depot and general store, water still dripped from the edge of the roof. Lyles Quinn and Jess St. Clair stood talking at one end of the porch. Sarah was combing the water out of her hair at the other.

Trudging through the mud from the saloon, Ned Guthrie approached.

"Hello, Ned," Sarah said.

Guthrie tipped the brim of his partially dried hat, "Ma'am."

"Turned out to be a little wetter than I thought," she laughed. "Only fools and newcomers, right? I qualify as a newcomer."

"Yes, Ma'am," the farmer said. Ned wasn't

much for talking to women. It was one of the things he never got the hang of.

Guthrie walked over to the other men.

"If it was just me, Lyles, I'd say sure let's give it another year," St. Clair said. "But it ain't."

"I understand," Lyles said as he looked up to see Guthrie. "Ned."

"Lyles," Guthrie said.

"Jess here says he's not sure he wants to buy any more seed."

"Can't blame 'im, can you?"

"No," answered Quinn. "But we're having some good rains."

"You still goin'?" Guthrie asked.

"That's why I'm here — waiting on the stage."

Jess St. Clair asked, "Ned, you plannin' t' stick it out another year?"

Ned Guthrie looked like he was closer to quitting than continuing, but he said, "Might."

"That's the kind of talk I like to hear," Quinn said slapping Ned on the shoulder.

"I ain't said nothin' fer sure."

"Come on inside and let me show you something. It's a seed catalog. Sarah, you comin'?"

"In a minute," she said still combing the last of the rain out of her tresses.

Quinn stepped over and they exchanged a small kiss.

After Quinn and the others had gone and Sarah had returned to running a comb through her hair, she saw something in the distance.

A rider on an Appaloosa came out of the distance toward town. He smoked a pipe and wore buckskins and tall boots. His coat was a thigh length buckskin with some fringe.

At the Elite Saloon, Hyer came out on the porch. He didn't notice the rider but focused his attention on Sarah.

She saw Hyer and didn't like his look. She turned and went inside the depot.

Hyer looked away and up the street. He saw the rider. Luther Bobbs looked up from his carving. He gestured toward the man on the horse and spoke to the young gunman.

"That's th' man you need t' talk t' about a job, young fella. Names' Zeak Thorndyke. Biggest rancher in these parts."

"Looks t' me like he's some kind 'a squaw man."

"Was once. These days he could buy an' sell th' both of us 20 times an' never miss th' change."

Dave Shambow pushed past Bobbs and hobbled out. He saw Thorndyke coming, too.

"Oh, hell." the stove up cowboy said.

He tried to straighten up and walk to the far side of the porch where he tried to hide his splint from Thorndyke. Luther Bobbs spat and almost hit Shambow on the foot.

"I got kicked by a jackass once," the old cowboy said. "Up in Montana Territory. I was stove up all winter. Hadn't been fer that ol' jackass I'd of died fer sure."

He paused and chewed a moment before continuing, "Either you fellas ever had jackass steaks? How about jackass ribs? Damn! I sure do miss that ol' jackass sometimes."

Thorndyke rode up to the saloon. He was 46 and clean shaven. But the marks of a hard life showed on his lined face.

Shambow greeted the rider, "Zeak."

"Luther. Shambow."

Thorndyke saw the splint on Shambow's foot.

"How long you had that, Shambow?

"Couple a weeks," the shabby ranch hand said. But he quickly added, "It's gettin' better."

Thorndyke frowned as he flipped his reins over the hitching post. As he loosened the Appaloosa's cinch, he said to Shambow, "Whose out at the line shack."

"Clovis."

"He doin' his work as well as yours?"

"We trade out. I jest come into town this morin'."

INSIDE THE DEPOT GUTHRIE PRODUCED A WAD OF rolled greenbacks. Reilly, the storekeeper, was behind the counter watching.

"There's thirty-two dollars here," Guthrie said. He handed the money to Quinn. "You best count it."

"Your word's good enough, Ned. If you say there's thirty-two dollars here — there's thirty-two dollars."

"Then I don't need no receipt. Jest give me your hand."

They shake hands.

"Thirty-two plus St. Clair's sixty-four, the Southwich's forty, the Ogan's twenty-seven plus Sarah and my fifty-six —I've got two-hundred-nineteen."

"You — you ain't carrin' a gun?" Guthrie asked.

"We don't own one — except for the rifle out at the place. I'm leaving that with Sarah."

"What you got there is 'bout all th' money I have in this world."

"It's also just about all the money we have in this world, too, Ned," Sarah said joining the conversation.

Guthrie pulled out a cap and ball pistol and handed it to Quinn.

St. Clair stepped up.

"You need a better gun than that." St. Clair said. "Here, Lyles. Use this." St. Clair produced a Remington 44. six shot cartridge revolver from the big pocket of his coat.

Quinn took the Remington and returned the ball pistol to Guthrie.

"How about a holster?" Reilly asked from behind the counter. He pulled up a used holster and belt. "This isn't fancy — or new — I took it in trade for somethin'. You can have it Quinn."

"Why would you give anything away?" Guthrie asked.

"I'm bettin' on you folks, too. If you stick an' do well — I'll do okay."

"I'll buy all the seed in a lot. Maybe we'll get a better deal," Quinn said slipping on the simple belt and holster. The .44 fit just fine. "Now, will you two see to it that Sarah gets home all right?"

"Of course," St. Clair said.

The sound of the stage coach arriving was heard. They all went outside.

# CHAPTER 4

The stage driver climbed down. He was wrapped in a yellow slicker but soaked through. His drooping hat hung down on both sides of his face. He handed a mailbag to Reilly before he turned to see the group.

"If'n any of you plan t' ride with me — you'd best not be in any hurry. I ain't movin' till I'm wrung out, dried out and fed up!"

"Your supper's waitin'," Reilly said.

With that the driver slogged past the group and went inside.

"You fellas want t' check th' mail?" Reilly asked.

"Sure," St. Clair said.

The men followed Reilly inside.

Luther Bobbs had crossed from the saloon. He stepped up on the porch behind Sarah.

"Ma'am," he said tipping his hat. "Thought you might like this."

He handed her the wooden horse he had just carved. It was still warm from his handling it.

Sarah was surprised as she examined the minutely detailed sculpture.

"This is lovely, Mr. Bobbs."

He didn't respond to her compliment but went to work changing the team of the stage.

❧

THORNDYKE STOOD AT THE BAR AS FENN finished pouring a drink.

"Stage's in," Fenn said. "This is th' third week you come in expectin' that Winchester. You sure it's comin'?"

Thorndyke swallowed his drink instead of answering.

The door opened and Hyer walked in and crossed to the bar.

"You, Zeak Thorndyke? Own a spread 'round here?"

Thorndyke eyed the young gunman.

"Who's askin'?"

"Name's Hyer. Willy Hyer. Ya' might a' heard a' me."

"Nope. What you fishin' for, boy? You know who I am."

"I hear you're short a line rider."

"What's that t' you?"

"I could use th' work."

Thorndyke looked Hyer over carefully.

"You don't look t' me like you've seen th' workin' side of th' sun in a coon's age."

Thorndyke reached out and took one of Hyer's hands and turned it palm up.

"Your hands been holdin' cards instead of rope an' pliers. My guess is you're better with a hand gun than you are with steers."

Hyer jerked his hand back.

"You sayin' I can't do th' job?"

"I ain't said I got a job."

"This time a' year you ain't gonna find many men lookin' fer work."

The rancher thought this over a moment.

"Can't do a thing for ya'."

"You're sayin' 'can't.' What ya' mean is 'won't.'"

"Young fella, Fenn tells me you already tried t' start a fight with a farmer."

Hyer threw a glance at Fenn who quickly busied himself.

"So? I got no love fer dirt eaters."

"They're here t' stay."

"I know some ranchers that b'lieve different."

"Twenty years ago the Comanches said th' same thing about ranchers. Lot of 'em died 'fore they got smart enough t' see it weren't no use. I don't plan t' make th' same mistake with farmers. I got no job for you."

Thorndyke finished his drink and walked out of the Elite Saloon. Hyer watched Thorndyke go with growing anger.

❧

LUTHER BOBBS BACKED THE FRESH TEAM INTO the stage traces. Quinn and Sarah were off by themselves. Quinn admired the wooden horse Sarah showed him while she read a letter.

"My sister's had her baby. A girl. She named her after Aunt Denise."

St. Clair and Guthrie stood a ways off minding their own business.

"I'm never going to like saying goodbye to you," Quinn said. "And I don't think I'll be very good at pretending I do."

"Then promise we won't do it much."

"Promise," he said putting his arms around her. "I'd feel a lot better if you would stay with the St. Claires."

"We settled that. I'm staying in my home -- our home. Maybe I'll finally be able to get some things done around there. All the things you haven't left me alone long enough to do," she said with a wink.

Quinn frowned. He didn't like to hear her joke about sex, at least not in public. She kissed his frown away.

"I'll miss you, Lyles."

"I miss you already."

Quinn released Sarah as he saw Thorndyke approach. Thorndyke tipped his hat to Sarah and nodded to Quinn. The buck-skinned clad rancher climbed up and looked on the top of the stage. Not finding what he was looking for he climbed down as the stage driver came out of the depot with a tooth pick in his mouth. He grinned.

"It's inside. On th' floor. Thought I'd try to keep it dry

Thorndyke opened the stage door and pulled out a long wooden box. He set his box down on some barrels by the depot. Thorndyke pried his box open with a Bowie knife from his belt. He pulled out a Winchester '73 rifle.

Luther Bobbs whistled.

"No wonder you been s' anxious. That's a beauty."

The Quinns, St. Clair and Guthrie also gathered around to admire the new rifle.

# CHAPTER 5

Hyer strode out of the saloon. He appeared with an angry expression. He saw the people over at the depot and he stepped out into the muddy street.

"Hey, Squaw man!" Hyer called.

Thorndyke slowly and methodically returned the rifle to the box before he turned to face Hyer.

Hyer started across toward Thorndyke who waited patiently.

The gunman spoke again, "I don't like askin'. But I'm goin' t' be real nice today an' ask you fer a job — one more time."

Thorndyke stepped into the mud, but there was no deadly snake-like slithering to his steps Hyer had.

"Is that what this is all about?" Thorndyke asked.

"Them your farmer friends there? I see th' *coffee coward* over there."

Guthrie swallowed hard and moved out of the way.

Quinn moved Sarah out of the way, ushering her toward the protection of the building.

Thorndyke faced Hyer in the street.

"I never did like boot lickers or sod busters," Hyer continued his taunt. "My ol' man was a sod buster. He weren't worth a damn." He took a breath before he said, "Now how about that job?"

"I got no need for a gunfighter."

"That's goin' t' be jest too damn bad. 'Cause I got no use for a squaw man."

Quinn felt the revolver in his belt but he didn't like the thought of using it. He looked around for an alternative and saw something.

Hyer moved around and Thorndyke countered him stepping away from the stage.

"You can even make th' first move, squaw man."

"I got no reason t' draw on you."

"Well, I'm goin'a kill ya, if'n you draw first or not. It don't make me no never mind."

The two men continued to move around staying opposite of each other. Hyer stopped when he neared the depot. The sun had come out and was then in Thorndyke's face. The rancher allowed his hand to drop slowly toward his revolver.

Quinn reached into one on the wooden barrels and pulled out a headless ax handle.

"Good-bye, squaw man." The gunfighter went for his gun.

"Hey!" Quinn called out as he flung the ax handle at Hyer's head.

Hyer cleared his holster with his pistol only to catch the ax handle right across his face. The gunfighter was knocked off his feet into the mud, his pistol flying.

Thorndyke was surprised. He expected to be shot. His weapon was only halfway out of his holster. He dropped it back into his leather. He stepped over and picked up the gunfighter's pistol.

Quinn crossed to Hyer who had blood streaming from his nose and from a cut across his forehead. Quinn picked up the ax handle.

Hyer opened his eyes and shook his head. He put his hand to his face.

"I'm bleeding! I'm bleeding!"

Thorndyke spun the cylinder on Hyer's pistol and dropped the bullets into the mud.

Thorndyke looked at Quinn.

"I owe ya '."

Quinn shrugged as if to say, it was nothing.

Thorndyke grabbed Hyer and lifted him to his feet.

"Luther," he said to Bobbs, "He got a horse?"

Luther Bobbs was near the stage. He crossed the street to a grulla hitched at the saloon.

"I'll get it."

As Bobbs stepped up to get Hyer's horse, Fenn came out on the porch of the saloon.

"Don't run him out till he pays what he owes."

"How much is that?" Thorndyke asked.

"'Bout a dollar and two bits."

"Thorndyke checked Hyer's pockets while shoving the young man through the mud. He found empty pockets. Thorndyke took the pistol and tossed it to Fenn.

"This'll have t' do."

"I'll kill you fer this," Hyer said to Thorndyke.

"Didn't you just try that?"

"Him, too," Hyer said towards Quinn. The blood was still streaming down the beaten man's face.

"Don't waste your time, son. I ain't worth killin'," Thorndyke said and then, nodding in Quinn's direction he added, "That man rode with Jeb Stuart. He can shoot the eyes out of a jack rabbit at a full gallop. You're lucky he didn't kill you."

Luther Bobbs met Thorndyke and Hyer in the

street with Hyer's horse. Thorndyke forced Hyer into the saddle and slapped the animal on the rump before Hyer could even get the bridle in his hands. The animal carried the gunfighter right out of town.

The stage driver climbed onto his seat.

"All aboard!"

Sarah had come back out and joined Quinn again. St. Clair, Guthrie and Reilly were there as well.

"Jess will see that you get home," Quinn said to his bride.

Sarah turned to St. Clair.

"That's sweet. Thank you."

"Of course," St. Clair said.

Guthrie added, "I'll go that way, too. Jest in case."

"I appreciate it," Quinn said.

He shook hands with St. Clair and Guthrie and then took Sarah in his arms for a good bye kiss.

Thorndyke came around the coach and went to get his rifle box. He looked to Quinn.

"Much obliged," the rancher said.

Quinn nodded and climbed on board the stage. Sarah blew him a kiss.

The stage pulled out and lumbered down the street in the opposite direction the Quinns had come when they arrived.

From inside the coach, Quinn looked back for one last look at Sarah.

St. Clair helped Sarah down and she sloshed through the mud to her wagon. Guthrie stood holding the horses as St. Clair helped Sarah onto the wooden seat. Guthrie tied his mount to the back of the wagon and got up beside Sarah. She gave him the reins.

St. Clair crossed over to his wagon, mounted it and followed Guthrie and Sarah down the street out of town.

Thorndyke headed for the saloon.

# CHAPTER 6

Tarr Phillips rode slowly, hunched down in the saddle, a bear of a man on a bone tired horse. The horse and rider came upon a road and turned to follow it. The horse and rider were oblivious to the passing stage which traveled in the opposite direction.

Quinn saw the figure outside his coach window. His eyes narrowed. There was something threatening about that man.

St. Clair helped Sarah down from the wagon at the Quinn place. It was a new house with a new barn and fences. It was a farm with hope and promise.

Ned Guthrie unhitched Sarah's horse and led him to the barn.

Sarah climbed the two steps to the front porch.

"Well, thank you, Jess — Ned, she said."

St. Clair had gotten down from his wagon to open the barn door for Ned. He waved his acknowledgment.

Ned returned to the wagon and got his horse.

Sarah stood watching when something caught her eye.

Tarr Phillips rode by as he continued toward town. He saw Sarah on the porch but nothing registered on his face. Still he continued to look at her as his horse walked on by.

Uneasy, Sarah sought the protection of the house, going inside quickly.

Guthrie looked toward the road and the rider.

Phillips was gone. But the sun was setting and evening was almost there.

❦

THE FOUR RIDERS, WHAT WAS LEFT OF FIVE FROM before, came down the muddy road. Like Phillips, these men and their mounts appeared to have come a great distance. These were hard men who were going beyond human endurance.

಄಄಄

INSIDE HER FARM HOUSE, SARAH WAS LOOKING at the wooden horse Luther Bobbs had given her. Sarah suddenly looked up as she got a chill. She bolted the front door closed and got the rifle from over the fireplace. She levered a round into the chamber. She sat it down near her rocking chair.

The four riders passed by the Quinn place without taking any note of the farm. They came and disappeared as if they were dark spirits from another world.

಄಄಄

THORNDYKE SAT IN A CHAIR NEAR THE STOVE IN the Elite Saloon, his new Winchester on the table in front of him. Fenn leaned on the bar while Shambow paced.

"I never said I couldn't do th' work," Shambow said. "I am doin' it. I'm goin' back to the shack. It's Clovis turn for a break. I'll be coverin' fer him like he done for me."

"You tellin' me you can do the work?"

Thorndyke asked. "All of it? Shambow, you ain't gettin' no younger."

"Oh, hell. I still pull my share."

Thorndyke thought for a moment before he spoke again.

"Tell you what I'll do. I'll send one of the other hands out to work with Clovis. You can work with me — long as you can keep up. Get on out to th' bunkhouse."

Shambow almost broke his neck stumbling to get on his coat and out the door. He bumped into Luther Bobbs who was returning from the depot in a hurry — a little out of breath.

"You won't believe what I jest seen! " Bobbs said to Shambow but also to those inside the saloon. "Comin' this way."

"What?" Fenn asked from behind the bar.

Bobbs stepped across to the window.

"Damn! He's comin' right in here!" Shambow said.

Fenn headed for the window himself.

"Who in th' hell are you talkin''bout?"

"Phillips. Tarr Phillips!"

"The Ranger?"

"I seen him once in San Anton. He took on the Effelberg brothers." Bobbs said as he crossed to the stove. "Both at the same time. Kilt 'em, too." The old horse wrangler waited there expectantly.

Fenn stayed at the window.

Only Thorndyke sat back undisturbed.

From the outside heavy footsteps were heard.

After a moment, the doors banged open and there was no one standing in the frame. The only sound in the saloon was the creaking of Thorndyke's chair. He calmly rocked back and forth.

The towering man finally stepped into the doorway. His wide brimmed sombrero sagged around Phillips' heavily lined and bearded face. In his arms outside his buffalo coat he cradled a large bore .10 gauge double barrel shotgun.

# CHAPTER 7

Texas Ranger Tarr Phillips scanned the room with his tired but sharp eyes. He crossed the room to the back door. He pulled it open, looked out, and then closed it. He snatched a chair and crammed it under the door knob, wedging it tightly in place. Then he crossed to the window.

Fenn made way for the big man and the barkeep worked his way back behind the bar.

At the window, Phillips paused and checked out the street. He then turned to glare at Thorndyke.

Thorndyke held the Ranger's look without blinking.

Phillips took a table near the back door, furthermost from the stove. His back was against the corner. He faced the front door.

He laid his .10 gauge across the table, drew two pistols and deposited them on the table, too.

With a look he communicated to Fenn that a drink was required.

Fenn moved quickly. He took a bottle from under the bar and a clean glass to Phillips.

Phillips fished a silver dollar from his pocket, flipped it to Fenn, who almost dropped it in his haste to get away and back to the bar.

Thorndyke stood and pitched a silver dollar onto the bar.

"Fenn," the rancher said, "I'll be on my way."

Phillips eyed the remaining men only a second before he poured himself an overflowing drink which he downed in a single swallow. He went to work on the pistols. Checking each he dried them off using a handkerchief which he had produced from inside his buffalo robe.

Thorndyke exited the saloon, taking his new rifle in its box.

Phillips pulled several shotgun shells from his belt and stood them on the table in a straight line. He poured himself another drink and waited.

Luther Bobbs stood near the potbellied stove and was apprehensive. Neither he nor Fenn wanted to miss anything significant, yet there was a strong sense that they could live a lot longer if they got the hell out of there. They were torn with indecision.

The sound of approaching horses was heard. Bobbs crossed to the window.

Phillips looked up at Bobbs.

"There's four of 'em," the old wrangler reported.

"There's gonna' be some killin' in here in about a minute," Phillips said. "You fellas might want t' get somewhere else."

Fenn and Luther exchanged looks and then did just as Phillips had suggested.

The two men from inside the saloon rushed out with their hands held up and stepped into the muddy street. They headed for the depot.

The four gunmen rode up in front of the saloon. They were all wearing slickers against the rain. They took them off and tied them behind their saddles.

The leader was Gus Fry, 58, ridden hard and put up wet way too many times. He had a cruel sneer, was unshaven with salt and pepper hair. He turned to the half-breed beside him.

"Round back," he said to Sam Deerinwater. The Indian was somewhere between 25 and 40. It was hard to tell. He had an emotionless face. He nodded and took his rifle with him toward the rear of the saloon.

Fry gestured toward one of the two remaining riders, Pete Guard, 43, a hard man with a mean look of a vulture about him. Fry motioned Guard toward the saloon. Next Fry looked at the Kid, maybe 16, scared but trying to hide it. The Kid was trying to learn how to be an outlaw.

"Back Sam up," Fry said

The boy took a breath and then slogged off to follow the half-breed.

While Pete Guard stood by the saloon's front door, Fry turned his horse and trotted across the street where he tied up his animal.

He pulled out his Winchester and crossed back to the other side of the Elite Saloon's front door.

# CHAPTER 8

Tarr Phillips heard footsteps on the boardwalk. Then they stopped. He took the shotgun shells one by one and inserted three of them between the fingers of his left hand. The one remaining shell he lodged between the second and third finger of his right hand.

Then he casually reached for his .10 gauge and aimed it toward the front door using the table to help steady the weapon.

There was a small metallic click at the back door. Phillips looked around the edge of the wall toward the rear door.

Some pressure was being applied to the door, but it was held fast by the chair. The knob turned back and then was still.

Phillips directed his attention now to the front door which opened slowly. Pete Guard, the hard vulture like man with one arm, appeared in the doorway. Phillips squeezed one trigger and his shotgun exploded.

Pete caught the blast full in the chest. He was lifted off his feet and thrown dead out onto the board walk.

The Ranger twisted in his chair, slipped his .10 gauge around, and fired at the back door. The door splintered and a man's dying scream was heard.

In a move surprisingly agile for a man of his age, Phillips bound up from his chair and lunged behind the bar where he hit the floor.

The Ranger broke open his shotgun, shook the expended shells from the breech and reloaded with two of the shells between the fingers of his left hand. The move was made with calculated ease. He had done this many times before. Then he was still, listening. There was only silence.

Phillips struggled to his knees glancing into the mirror behind the bar. He could see the open front door. Firing as he rose to his feet, he blew the Elite Saloon's lone window into the street. He rolled over the bar, fired a second covering blast at the gaping hole which had been the window, and made a running dive for the wall beside the jagged frame.

He reached inside his buffalo robe for more

shells but was stopped by the sound of running footsteps from the outside. A voice called from outside the saloon.

It was the kid. "Hey, Uncle Gus!! Wait!!!"

Phillips slung his shotgun away and dove out the window. Phillips slammed into the boards, rolling to a stop against one of the porch posts.

Gus Fry was mounting his horse across the street, leaning low in the saddle. He slapped leather while throwing wild shots back toward Phillips. The Kid rushed to his horse and clung to the saddle horn as his mount pulled free of the hitching rail and began to gallop out of town.

Phillips stood and fired both pistols — finally using the weapon in his right hand to throw three shots at Fry — but the outlaw escaped.

The Kid was in the saddle now, throwing shots toward Phillips as he tried to duplicate Fry's exit.

A chunk of wood was blown out of the post near Phillips' head.

He holstered one pistol and used both hands to steady the remaining six-shooter. He fired twice.

The young rider's horse went down, flipping the gunman headlong and screaming into the mud. The Kid's screams stopped abruptly as he smashed into the mud, his neck snapping on impact.

Phillips used his pistol again. He aimed and fired.

The body of the Kid jerked with the impact.

Then he crossed to where the Kid and the horse were sprawled in the street.

He reloaded the pistol in his hand as he stepped up and used his boot to kick the boy's body over violently.

The face of the young outlaw was spattered with mud. There was still innocence about it in death.

The Ranger had no reaction to this. He became aware of the slain gunman's wounded horse.

The beast thrashed about in unbearable pain.

Phillips softened and even shook his head a little. He raised his pistol and fired at the horse's head. The animal went still.

# CHAPTER 9

Phillips crouched beside the boy and went through his pockets. There were a few coins and a dollar or two which Phillips pocketed. He gathered up the boy's pistol.

Fenn was the first to step outside the depot. He was followed closely by Bobbs and then Reilly. They moved over and stood by the body at what was left of the front door of the saloon. They all stepped back as Phillips passed them on his way back inside.

The Ranger walked over and reclaimed his shotgun. Fenn, Bobbs and Reilly eased inside the wrecked saloon. Fenn struck a match and lit a lamp on the wall. Phillips went to his table as he reloaded his shotgun and took the bottle for a long drink.

Luther Bobbs was the first to speak. "You — uh — know these fellas, do ya'?"

"They're Gus Fry's trash. Fry got away."

Reilly, the store owner and depot manager said, "Gus Fry? Never heard of him. What'd he do?"

"Killed a man fer his boots in Ft. Worth. Then he stole a horse in Mineral Wells. I been after th' son-of-a-bitch for damn near two months."

The Ranger then led the way to the back door which had a big hole cut in it by buck shot.

"I heard of Fry," Luther Bobbs said. "But I thought Fry was from around Dallas. Didn't he get shot up tryin' t' rob a bank?"

Phillips kicked the chair away from the back door and then opened it revealing the twisted form of the half-breed. The Ranger stepped outside.

"This is Fry's new bunch. They're from around Big Springs. Th' one out here's that breed, Sam Deerinwater."

The lawman stooped and took the rifle from the dead man's fingers.

Next Phillips want back inside the saloon and crossed to the front door before he strode out to the plank boardwalk. The men followed him.

Phillips and the others stopped over the bloody

remains of the one armed drover. There was no weapon in his one exposed hand.

"This one's Pete Guard," Phillips said.

Phillips ripped open the man's long coat. Under it was the man's other, fully functional, arm. It was holding the butt of a vicious looking sawed off shotgun that hung by a strap from the outlaw's shoulder.

Phillips reached down into one of the outlaw's boots and extracted a dagger. Using the razor sharp blade, Phillips sliced through the leather strap and freed the over and under barreled shotgun. Then the Ranger went through Guard's pockets.

"How about th' kid out there?" Fenn the barkeep asked.

"'Spect he some kin of Fry's."

"Gus Fry'll be back. I heard of him, too," Bobbs said.

"Not till he's got somebody else t' do his head on killin' fer 'im. An' he's runnin' low on kin folk."

Phillips turned back into the saloon.

At the bar he laid down the arm load of weapons he had just collected. Fenn went around the bar and pulled out a couple of bottles and glasses.

To Fenn, Phillips said, "Say, Hoss, any law in this town?"

"Ain't needed any b'fore."

Fenn poured Phillips a drink as the Ranger put some money out onto the bar.

"Want Pete Guard's scatter gun?" Phillips asked.

"I got my own," Fenn said.

Phillips didn't like the sound of that.

Reilly reached for the shotgun.

Reilly spoke up, "If you're giving it away, I'll take it."

"I ain't givin' nothin' away, Hoss. But you can have the scatter gun and their hoglegs, too."

Suspiciously Reilly asked, "What's the deal?"

"Jest see that this trash gets put in a hole somewhere and covered up."

"Bury them?"

Phillips nodded.

"As long as it doesn't have to be anything fancy."

"Jest dig deep an' cover'em it over."

He pushed all the weapons toward Reilly.

"Who own's th' livery?"

Luther Bobbs answered, "The stage line. I run it."

"Their horses — the two that's left."

"I seen 'em."

"You interested in 'em?"

"They've almost been run t' th' ground."

"They're all good mounts. Check 'em over. They're yours fer $65."

Bobbs rubbed his chin, "That's a might steep."

"I ain't hagglin' over no damn horses. Take it or leave it."

"What's your rush?"

"Gus Fry," Phillips said. Then he added, "You got any women in this town?"

Fenn almost laughed. "Nope."

"Don't you bull shit me! I ain't nice when I get bull shitted."

"The kind of woman you're lookin' fer, mister, don't stay in little ol' smooth spots in th' road like this."

Phillips poured an overflowing drink and gulped it.

"About them horses?" Bobbs asked. "There's a couple of fair saddles there. You willin' t' throw in their gear?"

"Done!"

"Who's goin' t' pay for my damage. Front and back doors — window?"

"Bobbs pulled out a billfold, counted out the money for the horses and gave it to Phillips.

Phillips counted out a few of the bills and left them on the bar.

"That ought t' cover you — and a little extra for a couple of bottles."

Fenn produced 2 bottles of whiskey from the under the bar. Phillips filled his arms with the bottles and headed for the door.

# CHAPTER 10

The lights from inside the Quinn farmhouse were warm and inviting. Sarah came to the window and looked out. She measured the space for curtains. She was unaware that the shape of her body was visible through the gown to anyone looking in from the outside.

Sarah was not dressed or made up in any way which could be called sexy, attractive or tempting. She was merely a woman in her own house working while she was dressed for bed -- alone.

Inside her snug house, Sarah went to her rocking chair by the fireplace after writing down the measurements she'd taken on a piece of paper. She took up a hair brush and began brushing her hair 100 strokes as she did every night.

She continued her soothing motions until she felt a chill. She got up and stepped over to the kitchen wood burning stove.

Unseen by Sarah was a figure peering through the slats of the front door. The boards slightly obscured the view as Sarah took a few sticks from the wood box beside the stove and added them to the smoldering embers inside.

She blew the stove to life before closing the grated door. She reached for a tea pot and checked it for water. Finding enough there, she put it on the stove to heat.

A man's foot smashed into the door until it splintered and opened.

Sara was too startled to move except to look.

The figure of Willy Hyer stepped inside the door and he kicked it shut.

Sarah glanced toward the rocking chair and the rifle resting by it.

Hyer quickly rushed in and snatched up the gun before she could reach it. Hyer levered the rifle until all the shells fell to the floor. Then, holding the weapon by the barrel, he stuck it into the fireplace, giving it a final push which lodged it deep in the flames.

Sarah moved to put the table between herself and the intruder.

"Get out of here!"

Hyer began to advance on her. She moved to keep as much table between them as she could. He played the game for a moment, and then he flipped the table over, sending it crashing into the kitchen counter sending all of Sarah's sewing materials into the air.

She backed toward the stove and bumped into the tea pot. One of her hands went behind her and discovered a kitchen knife on the counter.

Hyer kept on coming. When he was close enough, she slashed at him. But he dodged the blow with surprising quickness and caught her wrist. He needed to apply only a little pressure to bend her arm and push her to her knees. Then he pried the blade from her hand.

Hyer thoroughly enjoyed the feeling of power this gave him.

He pulled her to her feet and shoved her into the bedroom.

Sarah was flung onto the bed, but she quickly rose and was now fully aware of his intent and her helplessness.

"Oh, please!! Please, God!!" she pleaded.

His response was to peel off his coat and remove his gun belt.

"Now this is the way it's goin' t' be, Missy. I'm goin' t' have you. There's nothin' you can do about it. But it's up t' you how you want it. It can be good for both of us, or it can only be good for me."

Sarah backed away from him against the far wall. Hyer sat on the bed and began removing his boots. That task done, he stood and removed his pants.

Sarah tried to flee through the door, but Hyer blocked her path. As he started coming out of his shirt and long handles, he stepped towards her again.

"You want 't take your clothes off," he asked with an evil grin, "-- or ya' want me t' do it for ya'?"

She turned away from him almost shaking.

Hyer stepped up behind her. He touched her arm and she jerked away.

"Last chance. Either you take 'em off or I will."

She couldn't respond to him.

"Want me to then?"

She managed to shake her head.

"Then get to it."

Hyer waited a couple of moments and when Sarah didn't move, he ripped the shawl from her back. She clutched at her nightgown.

She had her eyes closed as he took her arms, turned her around, and placed her hands one at a time, down at her sides.

Then he began to unbutton her gown. As he

did, Sarah started to tremble. He exposed her breasts and was mesmerized by her beauty.

As he pealed the gown from her shoulders and dropped it to the floor, exposing her completely, Sarah's knees buckled and she dropped to the floor throwing up.

A smashing of glass and an explosion thundered in the room. Hyer fell over on Sarah and she screamed. But in the moments that followed she realized that he was not moving. She struggled away from him and stood pulling her night gown back up her body. She shrank back from her attacker who now rolled over on the floor. A large, ugly and bloody hole was in his back.

She looked down at Hyer's blood on her. Then across the room she saw the face and smoking revolver of Tarr Phillips at the shattered window.

# CHAPTER 11

S arah clutched her bloody gown to her chest and raced back into the main room.

The front door was still ajar. Moments later the Ranger stepped through it, knocking politely as he came.

"Ma'am? You all right?"

She had re-buttoned her gown now and was huddled in front of the fire. It took her a moment before she could turn to the door and nod slightly.

"May I -- come in?"

He took out his Texas Rangers star and entered to bring it to her. He handed the badge to her. She studied the star in a circle in her hand and was able to nod a more assured understanding.

"Names, Phillips. Tarr Phillips," he told her.

He crossed to the bedroom while she remained by the fire. She heard Phillips moving about. It wasn't but a few seconds before Phillips returned from the bedroom. He had Hyer's body over his shoulder. Without a word he took the body out the front door.

Sarah turned to the fire and huddled holding her knees. She was shivering.

The Ranger returned a few minutes later and stopped to close what was left of the front door. He came up behind Sarah and stood there silently.

When he did finally speak he said, "You won't have to worry about him anymore."

Without facing her rescuer Sarah managed to say, "Thank you."

"It was somethin' that needed doin'."

She made herself turn and face Phillips. "I'm very glad you were here. Can I get you some coffee? Something to eat?"

He shook his head.

Through tears she said, "Well, I need some. I'll make it strong."

She turned and went to the stove while he righted the table.

"A woman like you shouldn't ought t' be 'lone out here."

"My husband's gone to buy seed." She worked

the pump beside the sink and got fresh water in the coffee pot.

"A woman 'lone, like you is temptin' to a man."

"I didn't do a thing. He broke in here."

"Don't have 't do nothin'. Jest bein' a woman, that's enough."

"I don't see why," she said adding coffee to the pot.

"That's just it. Women never do. Just shut up!"

"What?" she asked not understanding his change in tone.

"I said shut up. Why is women s' damn stupid?"

Sarah was suddenly afraid.

"Thank you for your help — but I think you'd better go."

"You want it. An' you know it."

"What?"

"You led him on, didn't ya'?"

"I did no such —"

"Jest like you're doin' me."

He grabbed her in a grip she couldn't escape from.

"Well, I'm goin' t' give you what you need."

"NO!!!"

She pulled back and threw his badge at Phillips. It fell to the floor. The horror of what had almost happened and what was about to happen again flooded Sarah. He slammed her down on the table as he ripped her gown from her body. She shrank away from him, but he grabbed her and violently back handed her across the face.

Sarah was stunned as he pulled her into the bedroom and flung her onto the bed.

Phillips removed his buffalo robe but didn't attempt to take any more of his clothes off. The mud and blood of his encounter with Gus Fry from before and with Hyer only moments ago were much in evidence. Sarah tried to get up but Phillips struck her again. Blood oozed from her mouth as she was stunned into submission. Phillips unbuttoned his pants before he climbed onto bed and mounted Sarah.

Tarr Phillips raped Sarah in a vicious, nonsexual, non-passionate assault. He used her brutally and savagely. He clawed at her, bit her flesh, penetrated her like an animal in heat — mauling her in every move.

When it was over, Phillips dropped across her limp body gasping for air, trying again to find the strength to continue. He was trying to reach a climax which eluded him. He finally gave up, exhausted but certainly not satisfied.

Sarah was a beaten, barely living creature. Her eyes were closed. She was marked with scratches and blood. She looked like an animal which had been badly injured in a struggle with another beast.

By then, the gray of dawn had replaced the dark of night but Sarah was still held in darkness.

Phillips pulled himself up, looked down at himself and then over at Sarah. He took part of a sheet and wiped some of the sweat from his chest and under his hairy arms. He blew his nose on the cloth before dropping it back where it had been. Then he buttoned up his pants and shirt.

Phillips came from the bedroom buckling on his gun belt with his huge buffalo robe under his arm.

He stood in the bedroom doorway, running his hand through his hair before he put on his sombrero.

"Don't make nothin' out a' this, lady. It don't mean a damn thing t' nobody. An' you ain't all that good, anyway!"

He turned to the front door and left.

Sarah was only vaguely aware of his words or of his going. But at the sound of the fading footsteps and the closing front door, she was numb to the world. She slowly opened her eyes but starred at nothing. She made no sound.

She was mentally and physically beaten. Her body trembled with small uncontrollable jerks. Her sanity and her humanity were clinging on with only a few fraying threads.

# CHAPTER 12

I t was a sunny day when all the farmers from the district awaited Quinn's return. His front yard was occupied when he arrived. Wagons, horses and mules were all over the place. Men and boys sat, laid on the ground and leaned against the wagon wheels and the barn.

Jess St. Clair and Ned Guthrie were at the hitching post directly in front of the house. The whole group looked up when one of the farm boys playing out by the gate with a couple of dogs, saw Quinn and shouted.

"Here he comes!"

There were three freight wagons, two loaded to the brim with sacks of seed. The third was filled with field plows, harnesses and other farming tools. Quinn drove the first wagon. He wore a tan corduroy coat and gloves. As he pulled up at the hitching post, the other wagons circled around by the barn.

Quinn was surprised at the crowd. "Whoa! This is some turnout," he said tying up his reins on the wagon's brake handle.

None of the farmers knew what to say. They stood uneasily. Then a few others gathered around the just arrived wagons, but they looked to St. Clair and Guthrie to take the lead.

Quinn began to sense that something wasn't right.

"Why so quiet? Look, I made an even better deal than I thought I could. We even have money left over. A little cash for everyone."

There was no response to this.

Quinn looked around and noticed that Sarah wasn't there.

"Sarah?"

Guthrie stepped up to hold Quinn back for a moment as he climbed down from the wagon seat.

"She's alive."

"Alive? Jess, what is it?"

St. Clair sighed and said, "Hold onto yourself, Lyles."

Quinn's attitude was suddenly ice cold.

"Tell me! Say it straight and quick!"

"My Anna and I were th' ones who found her," St. Clair said.

"Where?"

"Here. But she ain't talkin'."

Quinn pushed Guthrie away and got to the ground. He grabbed St. Clair by the shirt.

"Tell me, Jess! Now !!!"

"It, I mean, somebody, some man —."

Guthrie blurted out the news.

"She's been raped, Quinn."

Quinn flinched as if he had been stabbed. He tried to step back but was stopped by the wagon wheel behind him. He took a couple of deep breaths and got control of himself.

He pushed his way through the framers crowded there and moved toward the house. He mounted the steps and stopped before he touched the door. He noticed the door had been repaired with fresh wood. He lifted the new handle and went inside.

Before he could get more than two steps into the room, Quinn encountered Anna St. Clair, a strong woman who had aged beyond her years.

She was not content to merely step aside and allow Quinn to bull his way to Sarah who was sitting in her rocking chair by the fire, her back to him.

Quinn tried to step around Anna, but she

blocked his path. He caught sight of the bedroom. It was a wreck. He crossed to the bedroom doorway and looked in.

The bed was overturned. The mirror was smashed and the feather comforter slashed and scattered across the floor.

It hit him. This was where it happened.

Anna St. Clair said, "Lyles, the room was like that when we come."

Quinn looked down at Anna and then pushed her aside so he could get to Sarah. His young wife was rocking slowly, oblivious to anything.

Quinn froze. He couldn't seem to take another step.

"Sarah's been that way since we found her. She ain't slept in 'most a week. When she does, she wakes screaming."

Quinn moved slowly around the living room, without the force he had when he entered. He saw the damage which has been done to the table. He went to the side of the fireplace and picked up what was left of their rifle.

"She don't eat. 'Won't talk t' nobody. Jest sits there rockin' lookin' at th' fire. An', Lyles, she don't cry. I think that's bad. She's been hurt; terrible hurt. An' she don't cry. It scares me."

Quinn stepped closer to Sarah. He knelt down to her.

Her eyes were distant. The cut on the side of her head had scabbed over and was healing. Her cheeks were hollow. There were bags under her eyes and lines of age on her face which were not there when he left. There was none of the joy of life which he knew from before. She was all but a living corpse.

Anna crossed to the front door, took down her old coat off a peg and got into it. She looked back at Lyles and Sarah. There wasn't anything more for her to do. Anna opened the door and went outside.

Quinn held his position before he stood in front of the rocker for a couple of moments.

"Who did this, Sarah?"

She was unaware of him.

"Tell me!"

He shook her.

"Sarah?"

Nothing about her changed. He shook her again. This time he was more violent.

"Sarah! Who???"

She looked at him with a hint of recognition. Then she looked down at one of her hands.

She opened her clinched fist to reveal Tarr Phillips's Texas Ranger badge. It was blood stained from the force of her holding on to it so tightly.

Quinn took the object. When he looked into her eyes, he knew what she was saying.

# CHAPTER 13

Quinn stormed out of their farmhouse but stopped within a few steps. Anna St. Clair glanced at him before she went back into the house. Two of the other wives followed.

Some of the farmers and the teamster who drove the other wagon had begun the work of unloading the wagons. They had rolled back the tarps which covered the bags of seed on one wagon and the tools on the other.

Quinn crossed down to St. Clair and Guthrie.

"What was his name?"

St. Clair said, "We don't know."

"I say it was one of th' ranchers — or one of their hands," Guthrie said.

"Stop that, Guthrie. We don't know that."

"How about that body?"

"What body?" Quinn asked.

"One of th' dogs was diggin' it up." St. Clair said. "Out here."

Quinn followed St. Clair. Guthrie and some of the other farmers fell in behind them.

A shallow but open grave was behind the barn. A body, wrapped in a blanket had been uncovered.

Quinn stood looking down on the body. St. Clair and Guthrie were behind him. The other farmers circled around.

"One of the boys looking for his dog found it."

Quinn kneeled down and flipped back part of the cloth revealing a gray and slightly decomposed body of Willy Hyer.

"This is the gunslinger kid from town," Quinn said.

"It don't figure. If he done it, who killed him and put him here?"

Quinn flipped the body over and found the wound there. He dropped the corpse back and flipped the cover back over the body. Quinn stood up.

"Don't look a gift horse in th' mouth," Guthrie said. "Course he done it. What difference does it make who killed him? It's done. That's all that counts."

"He was shot in the back," Quinn said.

"And that could have been anyone," St. Clair said.

Quinn looked around. The other farmers were standing quietly.

"Any signs anywhere?"

"We've most likely covered up any sign since it happened. We didn't know this body was here until today."

"There has to be something," Quinn said searching the ground all around.

"What do you want sign for?" Guthrie demanded. "Your wife could have done this."

"We don't have any pistol in the house. That rifle that was burned in the fireplace was all we had."

"He's dead," Guthrie said. "Somebody done you a favor."

There was a long pause while Quinn glared at Guthrie. Finally it was St. Clair who broke the silence.

"Th' best tracker in these parts is Zeak Thorndyke."

Guthrie gave St. Clair a look of unbelievability.

"Nobody needs Zeak Thorndyke. I can follow sign."

"And you didn't see anything," Quinn said.

St. Clair spoke up, "Thorndyke's been fightin'

Comanche and livin' with Apache for most of his life. 'Member he's th' one who finally got that cougar none of us could find — two years back."

Quinn thought about this for only a moment.

"Jess, you mind if I hold on to your pistol a while longer?"

"Be my guest. But you should get a rifle if you're goin' hunting."

"Thanks," Quinn said as he stepped away.

❧

ZEAK THORNDYKE AND DAVE SHAMBOW, BOTH shirtless, were building a corral out of timbers in a small valley with a single opening. At the moment Quinn found them, they were trying to move a large boulder and straining in the process.

Quinn rode up, dismounted and lent his shoulder to the job. The large rock moved.

Shambow rubbed his splinted leg and sat down in the shadow of the boulder.

Quinn and Thorndyke spoke for only a couple of moments before Thorndyke grabbed his hat and shirt and went to his horse. He left a dumb-founded Shambow standing angrily alone.

Thorndyke mounted up and went with Quinn.

Shambow was so mad he threw his hat on the ground and kicked at it, only to miss and strike the boulder with his injured leg. He was bent over in pain as the two riders left.

❧

QUINN WAS STILL MOUNTED AT HYER'S GRAVE-site while Thorndyke knelt down to look at the ground.

Thorndyke examined the body and the grave. Jess St. Clair walked up.

"He's a big man — bigger than you." Thorndyke pronounced. "He's strong. Most of th' strokes he made with his shovel were deep."

Thorndyke led his horse to the front yard and kept looking at the ground.

The freight wagons had all been unloaded. The majority of the other farmers had left. Jess St. Clair and his wife Anna, who stood watching from the porch, were still there.

"He rode a big horse — and it carried a big load. That's about all I can see."

Quinn reached into his pocket and pulled out the badge. He handed it to Thorndyke.

"This mean anything to you?"

Thorndyke examined the badge. He looked up at Quinn.

"Name's Phillips. Tarr Phillips. He was through town the day you left."

Thorndyke gave the badge back to Quinn.

"Thanks. We're even," Quinn said.

"You plannin' t' go after him?"

Quinn nodded.

"I'll be goin' with ya'."

Quinn questioned this with a look.

"I'm goin' on my own account," Thorndyke said.

Quinn nodded approvingly.

"First light," Quinn said.

Thorndyke climbed back into the saddle and rode out.

Quinn dismounted and loosened the cinch on his saddle. He headed for Anna St. Clair who stood by the door.

"She's sleeping." she said to him when he stopped beside her. "I'll go home and get a few things. Go do what you have to. I'll stay here with Sarah."

"Thank you," Quinn said.

# CHAPTER 14

Q uinn and Thorndyke rode together across a broad flat expanse of Texas prairie. Each man was wrapped in his own thoughts. They were not so much together as they were riding a trail which was parallel to that of the other.

Thorndyke carried a pistol and had his new Winchester in a saddle scabbard. Quinn had only St. Clair's .44 revolver.

They reached a rain swollen river and had difficulty crossing it. They did manage the feat, but they did so each by himself, neither giving nor expecting assistance.

That night they sat on the ground in a camp on the trail. They were on opposite sides of their fire.

Thorndyke finished his meal of hardtack and reached for his pipe which he refilled and lit.

"It's that rain that saved us."

"How's that?"

"He left tracks in the mud. Th' mud dried an' left a trail."

"Mind my askin' why you're here?"

The rancher took a long draw off his pipe.

"Thought I might be some help."

"Course you are — but you didn't have to come. I didn't ask that of you."

It was a full minute before Thorndyke spoke again.

"My wife, a squaw by white man's ways, was killed by two or three men. They used her and then they scalped her. She was dead by the time I found her."

"Scalped?"

"Mexicans were payin' bounty for scalps; Injun scalps. Any Injun'."

He drew on his pipe and exhaled the smoke before continuing.

"Weren't no tracks t' foller. Still I tried. Spent a couple years lookin." Then Thorndyke turned the question back on Quinn. "Why are you here?"

Quinn didn't know how to answer this. The answer should have been obvious, he thought.

"I mean farmin'. Why out here? Even grass

don't grow too easy. One side a' beef per acre 'bout all it'll support. Can't be too good fer farmin'."

"My people have been farmin' Maryland since forever. That was good land. But we lost almost everything in th' war. My father mortgaged the whole place t' help finance a regiment for Lee. Th' Yankees didn't leave much standing when they came through. I went back for a while. My folks were both dead — I didn't seem t' belong anymore."

"So you started drifting. Happens after every war. You ended up out here?"

"One day I finally decided, I had t' get back t' workin' the land. It's the only kind of peace I've ever known. Really started out with nothing. But th' land was free. I don't mind hard work.

"But it's true we don't do much more than break even. Most of the rest are ready t' give up. I'm not much on quittin'."

"I've seen this land beat Injuns and Mexicans. It's killed more than a few whites."

"Not me."

"Sometimes leavin' ain't quittin'. You should'a learned that in th' war."

"Why'd *you* stay?" Quinn asked.

"My wife's buried here. So's my boy. If I'm lucky, they'll bury me here, too."

"You said you spent two years lookin' for those

men."

Thorndyke nodded.

"Why'd you stop?"

"Never found 'em."

"I would have kept lookin' till I did."

"Didn't make much sense after a while. I still had a son t' raise."

"I thought you said he was buried with your wife."

"He was 15 when he got caught in a stamped. He was 6 when they killed his mother."

"Didn't you want to get those men — for your son?"

"He needed a father more than I needed revenge. Findin' them, killin 'em, wouldn't make no difference. She was still dead. Nothin' I could do would change that."

"You sayin' I shouldn't be after this man?"

"I'm just tellin' you what happened t' me."

Thorndyke finished his pipe, knocked the ash out and pulled his hat down over his eyes as he laid back on his saddle.

Quinn leaned back on his and studied the night sky.

The heavens were a sea of countless diamonds from horizon to horizon.

THE NEXT DAY QUINN AND THORNDYKE WERE lost in the beginning of a dust storm. They both now wore slickers against the cutting grains of rock and dirt. They had their kerchiefs over their mouths and noses.

They battled their way through the storm for hours.

By dusk Thorndyke was leading the way. As Quinn came up beside Thorndyke, the rancher reacted to something in front of them.

Thorndyke peered through the dust. In their path there was the figure of a man, carrying a saddle.

Thorndyke looked back to see if Quinn was aware of the stranger ahead. Quinn saw the man, too.

The man carried a rifle in one hand and supported his saddle over his shoulder with the other. His slicker was tattered, his saddle worn, his hat dropping almost like a bonnet as he turned toward the two riders.

It was Gus Fry, the outlaw who escaped the gunfight with Tarr Phillips. Only his eyes hinted at the kind of man Fry was.

"Mornin', friend," Fry called out over the storm.

Fry let his saddle down and propped the butt of his rifle in his waist.

# CHAPTER 15

"A might bad fer walkin', ain't it?" Thorndyke asked.

"That it is. Blamed ol' mare went lame. Should 'a shot th' bitch, but I let'er go. You all come across 'er?"

"No," Quinn answered in a loud voice.

"Well, no matter," Fry said.

"If ya' can leave th' saddle," Thorndyke said, "we can give ya' lift t' th' next town."

"I do appreciate that. But th' next town's Waco."

"That's where we're headed," Thorndyke called through the wind. "T' Camp Fisher."

"Don't mean t' seem unneighborly, but I don't

have much love fer th' Rangers. Might say it's kind'a mutual."

"Then I reckon we can't help ya' friend."

Fry said, "You know th' ol' sayin', a man without a hoss is jest a foot."

Fry lowered the barrel of his rifle as he pulled back the hammer.

"I 'spect I'm goin' a have t' borrow one of your horses. That way I can get on 'bout my business."

"There's only one of you and two of us," Thorndyke said.

"An' you're thinkin' that ma'be I can only get one of ya'? 'Fore you go tryin' t' do somethin' stupid, ask ya'self, 'Have I taken care a' all my business?' Whoever th' one gets t' be — ain't ever goin' a get no more pie. Ever."

Quinn tightened his jaw.

Fry held his weapon steady.

"Now then, I fancy th' Appaloosa," he said indicating Thorndyke's mount. "Jest step down real careful like."

To Quinn the outlaw said, "An' you hold steady."

Thorndyke eased down off his horse keeping his hands out in plain view.

"Th' only reason I don't kill th' both a' ya' is 'cause ya did stop an' try to' be neighborly."

Fry waved Thorndyke away from his horse and Thorndyke moved.

"Now, you," he said to Quinn.

Quinn dismounted and crossed to Thorndyke, Fry reached and took the reins of both horses in his free hand.

"One at a time, now, I want ya' t' reach inside an' pull out them heavy ol' hog legs I know you're totin'. Mind ya' I want t' see fingers 'fore I see any metal."

Thorndyke produced his pistol and held it at arm's length.

"See jest how fer you can chunk it out there," Fry said.

Thorndyke tossed the pistol into the sand.

To Quinn Fry said, "Now you."

Quinn duplicated Thorndyke's action. Fry mounted Thorndyke's horse.

"There's jest one more little ol' thing I'll be needin'. You gents shed them boots."

Then both Quinn and Thorndyke sat down on rocks and pulled off their boots as the dust continued to blow.

"Toss 'em."

Both men threw their boots.

Fry made a mock salute, turned in the saddle and started to ride off — leading Quinn's horse behind him.

Quinn was ready for action but Thorndyke shook his head. Still, Quinn sprang like a cougar.

Quinn took three or four lighting steps and then vaulted into the air over the haunches of his own horse. The startled animal leaped forward as Quinn dropped in the saddle and slumped low as he snatched the reins from Fry's grip and spurred the horse away into the dust.

Fry was so rattled he only managed one wild shot. Quinn was gone and the startled Fry could do nothing but break into a gallop from the scene.

Still riding slumped over in the saddle, Quinn pulled his horse up short and listened. Over the sounds of the storm he heard Fry's mount galloping off. Quinn turned and took off back in the direction of Thorndyke.

Thorndyke moved off in search of their weapons. He located one and quickly spun the chamber and blew out the dirt. He was about half way through cleaning the gun when he paused to listen.

He heard the sound of one horse coming on fast. He switched to loading the pistol and went down on one knee to make himself a smaller target.

The rider came through the dust. Thorndyke leveled the weapon at the rider until he made out that it was Quinn. Then Thorndyke stood, did a road agent's switch and held the pistol out for Quinn. Quinn snatched it as he flew by and circled back at a full gallop in Fry's direction.

Thorndyke found the other pistol and repeated the cleaning process. He heard gunshots off in the distance.

In the dust storm, Fry was throwing wild shots behind him as he continued to ride aimlessly away.

Suddenly Quinn raced past Fry screaming a rebel yell and firing three shots in rapid succession. Fry caught one of Quinn's slugs in the arm and fumbled his rifle away.

Fry regained his balance on his fast moving mount and leaned forward clutching his wounded arm. He was able to get his pistol out, but the pain from the bullet wound was intense.

He slowed his horse to catch his breath and listen for Quinn while he looked at his arm. It was a serious injury.

He tied off the wound with the scarf from around his neck and moved on. He heard a rebel yell again, from behind, turned and fired, but there was nothing back there.

The sound of Quinn's horse was there and it faded. There was no physical evidence that Quinn was there.

Quinn's horse was heard again. This time at Fry's right. The outlaw threw more wild shots as the hooves faded off.

He spun in the saddle, first to one side, then behind him, then the other side. Nothing.

# CHAPTER 16

A dilapidated adobe line shack, long abandoned, materialized out of the blowing dust. Fry spurred Thorndyke's' Appaloosa toward it. He all but fell out of the saddle and crashed into the building.

He was breathing at an alarming pace but tried to control it. He listened. Nothing but the storm was heard.

He pulled the horse to the door of the structure and whipped it into the cabin ahead of him. He ducked into the building.

Fry huddled in the corner for the safety of the dim interior. Then the world caved in on Fry and he crumbled in a heap to the dirt floor. Behind him was Quinn standing in the shadows. He had pushed over the adobe wall protecting Fry.

❧

A BRANCH WAS STUFFED INTO THE HOTTEST PART of a wood camp fire. Then the branch was pulled out, still burning. The flame died away and the smoking end of the branch was stabbed into the swollen and bruised flesh of a bullet wound. The flesh sizzled.

Thorndyke was holding the limp body of Fry as Quinn expertly seared the wound closed. Fry came to, yelling in pain as Quinn continued holding the embers of the stick in place. Thorndyke struggled to keep Fry down. Finally Quinn was through and backed off, flipping the stick back into the fire. Thorndyke released Fry allowing him to grab his injured arm.

"He'll live," Quinn said.

"Damn you to hell!!! What did you do to me? Give me some grease or somethin'."

"There ain't nothin'," Thorndyke said.

Fry pulled his shirt back over his shoulders.

The line shack barely stood. There was a little of the remaining roof over them and a rear room where the horses stood hobbled.

The storm had passed and a small fire blazed on the dirt floor.

Quinn went back to the animals and began to brush them. Thorndyke tied Fry up, keeping the injured arm in a sling but roping it securely in place.

Thorndyke next set about the task of preparing an evening meal. Fry eyed the food hungrily. His eyes also took note of the Bowie knife stuck in a log only a few feet away from him.

"I guess I ought t' thank you," Fry said trying to deal with the pain. "But I ain't sure I want to. Where'd he learn t' ride like that?"

"You'll have t' ask him," Thorndyke said.

Fry twisted around to speak to Quinn.

"Say, where did you ever learn t' ride like that?"

Quinn just looked at Fry for an instant before he went on about his business.

"I'd bet it was with Jeb Stewart."

Quinn didn't answer.

"Only men I ever in my life seen that could handle a horse like that were rebs." He paused and then said, "Course some did ride with Quantrill."

Quinn stopped brushing his horse but would not even turn toward Fry. He went back to work.

"Say, friend, I ain't sayin' you rode with Quantrill. Hell, if ya' had, I'd a' knowed ya'."

"You'd best shut your mouth," Thorndyke said.

Fry did as he was told — but only for a moment.

"Them beans smell good," he said. "I ain't had nothin' t' eat in three days. It'd be th' Christian thing t' do, feedin' a poor fella' like me."

"Like you was goin' t' feed us to th' coyotes?"

Quinn returned to the fire. He and Thorndyke exchanged looks.

"I think we could let him eat. Without his hands."

Fry started to protest, "Say, there —"

"Or not at all," Quinn added.

"What th' hell."

Thorndyke dished up the beans and gave the first plate to Quinn who accepted it with a nod. Quinn sat and started to eat. To Thorndyke he said, "I'm sorry about your wife."

Thorndyke looked up and said, "It was a long time ago."

"But still," Quinn said.

"Th' hard part for you is still ahead. After we're through with Phillips, you and our wife still got t' live with it."

"You ain't talkin' 'bout that bastard Tarr Phillips, are ya?" Fry asked, his mouth watering at the plate of beans Quinn and Thorndyke were eating.

Quinn turned to Fry.

"Oh, I know 'im. We rode t'gether a few years. That's right. Then he put on that badge and got s' damn high n' mighty. Hell, I know all 'bout him. I also know what he likes t' do with women."

"Shut your damn mouth," Thorndyke said.

"Jest try'in t' help. Ya' know, he's been thrown out of every cat house in South Texas. Ol' Katy Page's place in Corpus is 'bout th' only place he can still get in. Course he'd rather take his fun with somebody else's wife if he could."

Fry saw that he had hit a nerve.

"More than one husband's tried t' geld ol' Tarr. Ain't none made it, yet. 'Somebody ever does, there'll be lots of sad women in Texas. That ol' Tarr's a ring-tail tooter."

Quinn got up and walked away.

❧

LATER WHEN THE OUTLAW WAS FINISHED EATING from a plate on the ground, he wiped his mouth off on his clothes as best he could.

"I do say thanks fer the food."

"The less you say the more apt you are to keep breathing," Thorndyke said.

"Look, pard, if there's one thin' in this world I knows, it's women. Let me tell ya' this, there ain't never been no woman that got it that didn't want it."

Thorndyke reached across and backhanded Fry, flattening the outlaw on his back. But Fry was aware that Quinn was listening. With a dribble of blood coming out of the corner of his mouth, Fry laid there and went on talking to Quinn.

"I ain't jest talkin'. Look, I can show you."

Fry tried to get back up as Thorndyke moved toward him again.

"Wait a minute," Quinn said.

"I can prove what I say," the outlaw muttered.

"Like horse shit, you can," Thorndyke said.

"I ain't lyin'. You cut me loose an' I'll show ya'."

# CHAPTER 17

There was no interest on either Quinn or Thorndyke's part to free Fry.

"You two ain't scared are ya'? Look I got a hole in one arm. Jest let me have my good arm loose. Hell, there's two a' ya'."

"What do you mean you can prove it?" Quinn asked.

"Free up my arm and I'll show ya'. Then you make up your own mind."

Quinn finally moved. He pulled out his pistol and stepped over to Fry, untying the arm Thorndyke had knotted behind the outlaw.

Thorndyke moved off not believing this was happening.

Quinn stepped back keeping his pistol leveled at Fry.

The man reached slowly for a coffee cup.

"Can ya' grab that pot there?" he said to Quinn. Fry indicated the pot of coffee which now boiled on the open fire.

"You said you had something to show us."

"This is part of it."

Quinn sighed and reached for the coffee pot with a rag in his hand.

"Now, let's jest say that this here cup is a woman. 'Least, th' best part a' one. An' let's say that pot of coffee's a man that's 'bout t' bust jest t' get him a little. Now, you pour me a cup."

Quinn questions this a moment an still began to pour some hot coffee into the cup. But Fry moved his cup at the last moment. The coffee spilled on the ground. Quinn tried to pour again and once more Fry kept the cup out of the path of the liquid. Then he holds still and Quinn poured some coffee into the steady cup.

"See, there ain't no way. You can't get your thing in, lest I really want you t'."

Quinn was struck to his soul. He sat the coffee back on the fire and stepped away disturbed.

"That's th' way it's always been. 'Course ain't no little bitch ever goin' a admit it."

As Quinn moved off, Fry sat down his cup and

inched toward the log where the bowie knife awaited invitingly.

Fry's hand went for the handle of the knife, but Thorndyke's boot crashed down on Fry's wrist pinning it to the log. Then Thorndyke reached down and extracted the blade.

Thorndyke grabbed Fry by the collar shoving the blade of the pig sticker dangerously deep into the flesh of Fry's throat without breaking the skin.

"Don't even take a deep breath, boy! Or you'll drown in your own blood!"

Thorndyke released Fry's shirt but the outlaw remained frozen where he was. The rancher reached back for the cup Fry dropped. He jammed this back into Fry's hand.

"Move this," Thorndyke said, "even an inch and I'll slit your gizzard!"

Thorndyke reached back into the fire with the rag protecting his hand, and brought the pot of coffee back to the cup.

"Let me see if I can 'get a little' in your cup."

Thorndyke eased the blade deeper into Fry's throat breaking the skin slightly, Fry's eyes were wide with fear.

Thorndyke began to pour the steaming brew. He slowly filled the cup. But he did not stop.

Fry cut his eyes to the cup, realizing what was happening.

The level of the coffee rose to the lip of the cup and began to spill over.

Fry flinched as the boiling liquid gushed down his wrist and arm scalding skin as it went.

Thorndyke continued to calmly pour.

Fry screamed through clenched teeth. Tears streamed down his face.

Finally, Thorndyke stepped back releasing Fry and tipping the pot up right.

Fry dropped the cup and doubled over in pain. Thorndyke slipped the knife back in his belt.

Quinn understood.

Thorndyke looped the rope around Fry again and gave it a pop to tighten it.

۞

THE ROPE AROUND FRY JERKED HIM ALONG behind Thorndyke's horse in the morning light. The outlaw stumbled through the rocks on the trail. Quinn rode beside Thorndyke.

They rode down the dusty trail which led to the main gate of a military post. The weathered sign swinging in the wind read, CAMP FISHER — TEXAS RANGERS.

Fry stumbled almost in a trance, weary from many miles of walking. The trio passed through the gate at the signal from the guard on duty.

"We've got a prisoner for you," Thorndyke said.

"You'll find Sgt. Goode in th' barn. Straight back," the young man said.

The ranger headquarters looked like an Army fort. A drill field was a sea of dust. Around it were buildings which were obviously barracks, guard house, mess hall, infirmary, administration and at the rear, a corral and barn. The doors to the barn were open.

As Quinn and Thorndyke rode across to the barn, they noted the few men around the compound. There were no uniforms for these men. The only consistent item of clothing was their Texas Ranger Star.

One man sat in a chair platting strips of leather into what looked like a bull whip. Another was cleaning a rifle.

# CHAPTER 18

Quinn and Thorndyke rode up to the barn but stayed in the saddle. Fry dropped to the ground.

In the barn was a group of rangers working in the shade and tending to the horses. The older man was supervising the younger men. Sgt. Daryl Goode, the oldest ranger had a commanding presence. He looked at the prisoner in the dirt.

"Gus Fry. Well, how'd you come by him?" Sgt. Goode asked.

"He tried to 'borrow' our horses," Thorndyke said.

"Yeah. He has a way a' doin' that. Looks t' me like you all kind of changed his mind." To both men Sgt. Goode said, "Step down. Sherman, take their horses."

A young Ranger put down his broom and took Quinn and Thorndyke's horses."

"Captain Luke'll want 't see you," the Sgt. said. "Come this way."

Quinn and Thorndyke followed Goode across the parade ground.

"There might even be a reward fer Fry, you know."

Quinn spoke for the first time.

"We are not bounty hunters."

"Didn't mean t' say ya' were."

The trio mounted the steps of the headquarters building.

The door of the building opened before they could reach it. Out stepped a stocky and muscular man in a clean shirt and shiny badge. Stamped into the metal were the words Captain — Texas Rangers.

"Captain, these fellas just brung in Gus Fry."

"Fry?"

"Yes, Sir." Sgt. Goode gave a casual salute and headed back to the barn.

"Captain Billy Luke." the officer said extending his hand.

"Captain. I'm Zeak Thorndyke."

"Mr. Thorndyke, it's a pleasure."

Luke offered his hand to Quinn but Quinn did not take it. Thorndyke did the introduction.

"This is Lyles Quinn."

The captain dropped his hand.

"All right, Mr. Quinn. Step inside. I think the State of Texas owes you gents."

"We're not interested in any bounty," Thorndyke said.

"How about at least a drink?"

Thorndyke and Quinn follow Captain Luke into the building

They crossed an outer office to one with the name CAPTAIN LUKE on the door. Boxes overflowed with papers. The few bookcases sagged under the weight of too many books, records and more papers.

The captain uncovered a half full bottle of whiskey from one of the shelves. He searched his desk drawers for glasses.

"Make yourself t' home."

"We're in a hurry, Captain," Quinn said.

Still looking for his serving glasses, Billy Luke said, "I know th' damn things are 'round here somewheres."

Thorndyke stepped across to the window and looked out. The rancher saw two rangers following Sgt. Goode, dragging the limp body of Gus Fry. They were headed for the guard house.

"If we ever lose Texas, it's goin' to be t' politicians and paper work," the Captain said.

He found the glasses under a stack of paper.

"Here they are."

He poured three glasses and offered them to his guests. They all drank. Then Quinn pulled out Phillips' badge and dropped it, blood stains visible, onto the captain's desk.

"Where can we find Tarr Phillips?"

"What do you want with him?"

Quinn held the Captain's gaze.

"Where?" Quinn asked again.

"You ain't answered me, yet. What's your business with Tarr?"

"Captain, there's no law says we have t' tell anybody our business."

"There's no law says I got t' tell you where t' find him, either."

"It's between us," Quinn replied.

The captain sat as he said, "There have been others t' come lookin' for him b'fore. They come back tied across their saddles. Tarr Phillips is a hard man."

When neither Quinn nor Thorndyke responded, the captain went on.

"What is it with you? He bust your fence? Shoot a hole in your brother? Run off with your horse? Tell me what it is and I'll pay the damages. It'll come out of his pay."

"Somethings money jest can't fix," Thorndyke said.

Luke looked at the map on his wall. He pointed to it.

"Ya' know, Texas is one hell of a big place. You fellas' got any idear what it's like t' bring law an' some kind a' order t' all this?"

The two men said nothing.

"I guess not. Who does? Who even gives a damn?"

Quinn was unmoved.

"Third time. Where?"

Luke sighed.

"Everybody wants law and order till it's their ox that gets gored. Then, th' hell with it. Grab a rope an' string th' bastard up t' th' nearest tree."

The Captain rubbed his head wearily.

"I know what Phillips is. For a long time he was what Texas needed. There's been times when he's been th' only thing between a man gettin' a fair trial or a lynch mob. He's fought Comancheros, Apaches, robbers, killers."

"Times change. So does Texas," Thorndyke said.

"If you've got a quarrel with him -- make it legal. Swear out a complaint."

Neither Quinn nor Thorndyke spoke.

Finally after a long moment of silence in the office, Captain Luke said, "The warrants he had were for Gus Fry — and then Willis Sisyk. Th' last time Sisyk was seen was 'round Corpus Christi."

Quinn turned to the door and left. Captain Luke faced Thorndyke.

"Mind tellin' me what it's all about?"

"His bride."

"If it makes any difference, she ain't th' first."

"Ma'be she'll be th' last."

"All he's going to do is make her a widow."

"Don't you bet on it."

"If you two get lucky and somehow manage t' kill Phillips instead of bringin' him back here, we'll be after you."

"Seems like you've knowed about him for a long time and you ain't done nothin' about it. It's time somebody did."

Thorndyke walked out.

When Thorndyke was mounted up beside Quinn, the two rode out the gate of Camp Fisher as Captain Luke stepped out onto the porch. Sgt. Goode came up as the two Rangers who had helped with Fry headed back to the barn.

"Doc Gully says Fry'll live long enough t' hang."

The captain spat in the dirt.

"Sgt., I need you to send a telegram."

# CHAPTER 19

A driving rain obscured the muddy street as thunder rolled overhead. A young tele-graph carrier, 9 or 10, raced across the busy street and past a sign which swung in the rain. In front of a large and imposing house, the sign read, KATY PAGE'S PUSS n' BOOTS PALACE.

The front door opened before the youngster could get there. A middle aged black woman held the door open as a young white man, early 30's stepped outside. He had a sample case in his hand and a shit-eating grin on his face.

"Mista Keith, we goin' a be lookin' t' sees you all again. 'Course th' girls is already sayin' things ain't goin' t' be da' same till you gets back."

The man's grin broadened and almost split his

face as he left. The woman was about to burst with her own laughter as soon as his back was turned, but she managed to control herself. The telegraph boy tried to dart through the door, but the woman casually lifted him off his feet by the back of his collar.

The woman was dressed in black with a white apron. She looked to be a maid of a wealthy family.

"Jest where's them little fat legs carrin' you, boy?"

"I have important business," the boy said.

"It had better be."

She closed the door.

Inside the house the woman switched her grip from his collar to his ear and dragged him past the parlor where he got only a glimpse of the scantily clad young women of different races, hair colors and shapes. They were all drinking, singing and entertaining a small group of men, all of whom were dressed in shirts and ties.

The black woman ushered the boy back beyond the stairs. The boy had evidently heard a lot about *upstairs* because of the way his eyes almost popped out trying to see something up there.

Before they could reach the door to the kitchen, it opened and out stepped Katy Page, a very faded flower who tried to hide behind too much make-up what age and her profession had done to her looks.

"What in th' world?" Katy said looking at the boy.

She followed the boys gaze up the stairs.

The black woman said, "He has *important bin'ess'* — he says."

"Looks to me like he's window shopping."

"I have a telegram here," he said.

The boy produced the message from his pouch.

Kate reached for it, but the boy pulled it out of her reach.

"Telegram? For who?"

"Mr. Texas Ranger Tarr Phillips."

Katy reached for the message again. "Let me see that."

"No, ma'am. I was told to deliver it right into his hands."

Katy made a shrug and turned away only to whip back and snatch the envelope. The boy tried to reach for it again, but the black woman held him back.

The boy was on the verge of tears. "Please, ma'am. I'm not supposed to let that out of my hands."

"Tell you what. You leave this with me, an' I'll see that Mr. Phillips gets it."

"No, ma'am, I can't do that."

"You see, son, Mr. Phillips is tied up right now."

The black woman said, "More likely Miss Una's th' one tied up."

"I'm supposed to put that right in his hands. Myself."

To the woman Katy said, "Why don't you take this young man up stairs?"

Those magic words made the boy's mouth fall open.

"See if you can't find him a place t' watch for a while." To the boy she said, "You can tell your boss you had to wait a bit before you could see the Ranger."

"Yeah!!" the boy agreed.

The black woman led the boy off but he turned back.

"If there's a tip, you'll save it for me?"

"Of course. Now, enjoy yourself."

The black woman started up the stairs with the boy right behind her. He was so busy looking, he almost tripped on every other step.

When Katy was sure the boy was otherwise occupied, she slit open the envelope with the edge of one of her knife sharp fingernails. She carefully pulled the message out, unfolded it and read it.

TEXAS RANGER TARR PHILLIPS
CORPUS CHRISTI, TEXAS

JACK R. STANLEY

C/o KATY'S PUSS 'N BOOTS PALACE
    TWO  MEN  THROUGH  HERE  TODAY
LOOKING FOR YOU - STOP - ONE IS MAD
HUSBAND - STOP - A FARMER - STOP - A
RANCHER WITH HIM - STOP - NAMES ARE
QUINN AND THORNDYKE - STOP
    CAPTAIN BILLY LUKE

# CHAPTER 20

K ate threw the torn telegraph envelope into a trash can. There was a writing desk/secretary in the hall way beside the stairs. She opened the lid and let it fall down as a writing table. She pulled open a small drawer and extracted a clean, official telegraph envelope. She inserted the message, readdressed it and then sealed it.

Katy stepped over to the parlor door, caught one girl's eye and motioned to her. A classy redhead, dressed in a dark green corset, stockings, and short lace-up boots, left the gathering and went to Kate.

"Crystal, I want you to take this up to room 27."

Crystal took the telegram and without examining it starts up the stairs. She took only one step, however, before she stopped and whipped her head back to Katy.

"Wait just one little minute. Twenty-seven? Ain't that where that damn Ranger is? I'm only now getting over th' last time I had somethin' t' do with that bastard."

"All I want you to do is deliver the telegram. Nothing more — nothing less."

Crystal reluctantly turned and climbed the stairs.

She walked down a long hall of flocked red wall paper and red colored lamps. Crystal stepped up to room number 27. She listened and then she knocked.

"Yeah?" came Tarr Phillips voice through the door.

"There's a telegram. For you."

"So?"

"Kate wants me t' give it to you."

"Well, get in here."

Crystal opened the door and stepped inside.

The big Ranger was in bed, naked but with a pillow covering his crotch. He still had his boots on. He held a cocked pistol level with the door. Beside Phillips in bed, was Una, a slinky, Mexican whore who was smoking a cigar and making no attempt to cover her nakedness. Her left eye was swollen badly, but she ignored it.

Crystal stood inside the door, eyes on the gun, afraid to move.

"She all right, Señor. She is Crystal."

Phillips slipped his weapon back in the holster which hung on the brass head board.

Phillips said, "I 'member you from —"

"I haven't forgotten it either," Crystal said.

"I'll bet you haven't. But I pay for my fun."

Crystal stepped toward the bed and handed the telegram to Phillips. He took it and discarded it over on the bed. At the same time he slipped a hand on Crystal's buttocks.

"Come on an' join in."

"No, thanks," she said curtly removing his hand. "I've already been."

She crossed back to the door, opened it but turned back to Phillips.

"What are you going to do about the telegram?" she asked.

He picked up the envelope and ripped it in two.

"Aren't you even going to read it?"

"I don't like readin'." Then to Una he said, "You?"

Una merely made a disgusted face.

Phillips said to Crystal, "How 'bout you?"

"I never found readin' t' be much help in my line a' work."

Crystal stepped out and closed the door. Phillips took a handful of Una's breast and moved over on top of her as she continued to smoke. It was as if she were somewhere else in her mind, totally unaffected by what was happening to her body.

When Crystal reached the bottom of the stairs, Katy stepped forward.

"Well?"

"Well, what?"

"What did he say?"

"He tore it up. Oh, and you'd better get Doc for Una. She's going t' need it."

❦

QUINN AND THORNDYKE WATERED THEIR HORSES at a clear river crossing.

"Given much thought t' what you'll do if we get lucky?" Thorndyke asked.

"Lucky?"

"An' get Phillips. Say we kill him. Then what?"

"Then it's over. We go home."

"What do ya' do when you get home?"

"What are you getting at?"

Thorndyke was silent a moment before he

spoke again. "That's what you've been running away from. What you're going t' do about your wife? What are ya' goin'a say?"

Quinn hadn't thought about this and didn't want to now. Thorndyke shook his head sadly.

"This won't be over — for you — or for her. Not by a long shot."

# CHAPTER 21

Thorndyke and Quinn loosened their cinches and allowed their horses to graze by the flowing river. The men found the shade of a large live oak and sat down to rest themselves.

After a few minutes of silence between the two men, Thorndyke spoke as he pulled out his pipe.

"I come up on some Comanche once, back when I was scoutin'. They was down by some river. I knew they had t' cross it and so did I. Comanche's mean. They was jest breakin' camp — but somethin' was goin' on. Now I knew 'bout enough Comanche t' get m'self in trouble, s' I stayed back in th' rocks an' listened."

Thorndyke filled his pipe and lit it.

"Seems some young buck had — taken his pleasures with the wife of another brave. The whole tribe was all riled up.

"The brave and the squaw were grabbed and tied up. Then they were bound together. The brave and the woman were carried over to the edge of the river. The whole tribe watched.

"Th' way they saw it, whenever somethin' like that happens, it ain't jest th' man's fault. Th' woman's ever bit as guilty. Then they toss 'em in th' nearest river or lake t' drown.

"Another brave comes rushing up. He goes to the woman. I figured he was her husband.

"But th' thing is, th' husband can go in an' save his own wife if he wants t'. It's up t' him. 'Course if he does, if he goes an' gets her, then it's all right fer somebody t' go in an' save th' man, too.

"The brave pulled out his knife and had to be held back by others in the tribe. He wanted to kill the man bound to his wife.

"This woman was cryin' an' screamin'. He had t' be held back from tryin' t' cut up th' young buck. Now, th' buck was standin' there not makin' a sound. I kind'a thought he was ready t' pay fer what he done. 'Course ya' never know with Injuns."

Thorndyke took a long draw on his pipe before the continued with the story.

"The husband kicked off his moccasins and readied himself to dive into the water.

"He *said* something 'bout swimmin' t' th' woman. That seemed t' calm her down some. He stripped ever'thing off and ran up there beside th' river t' wait.

"They got ready t' throw 'em both in when this ol' man got up there next t' th' husband. He peeled off and was ready t' go in, too. I figured he was th' buck's ol' man, or somethin'. Both of 'em had their knives in their teeth an' was ready t' dive.

"The bound couple was thrown into the water by several of the men in the tribe. They went under but come up for air a moment later.

"An let me tell ya' th' tied up buck decided right quick that he didn't want t' die after all. Both of em started kickin' an' screamin'. She was hollerin' fer her man t' jump in. They was all watchin' th' husband. I guess nobody could go get th' buck till somebody went after th' woman first.

"They was fightin' fer air, by this time — goin down fer th' second 'r third time. I tell ya', that ol' man was 'bout t' bust t' get in there an' get that buck.

"Then the husband stepped back from the river's edge. He picked up his clothes an' got dressed. Th' ol' man had t' give up, too. They jest let 'em both drown, t'gether."

Quinn sat listening as the rancher finished his story.

"Th' tribe packed up and rode off. Didn't even go after th' bodies. Th' husband never looked back. Guess he wanted t' get even more than he wanted his wife."

Thorndyke was finished with his pipe. He knocked the ashes out of the bowl and put the pipe back in his coat pocket.

The story struck Quinn to the quick. He looked off into the distance.

There, clouds were gathering and thunder was heard far off.

# CHAPTER 22

On a dockside street in Corpus Christi, thunder rolled and the howl of a powerful storm lashed Quinn and Thorndyke.

The two searchers were on horseback, both wearing slickers, their hats blown flat against their heads. A few citizens rushed across the street. Some carried boxes or belongings of some value.

A building they passed bore a sign: CORPUS CHRISTI PORT STORAGE.

The riders finally reached the point where it was no longer possible to ride into the growing fury of this onslaught. Both men dismounted and took the reins in hand to lead their frightened horses on.

There were a couple of men struggling to keep their balance as they attempted to board up a store window. Most of the windows and doors were already boarded up on all the buildings.

As a man passed in front of Quinn, the rider reached out to stop him. The man said something which Quinn could not make out. The man pointed to the sky. He said the word "hurricane" twice.

The man pulled away and hurried off.

Quinn and Thorndyke rounded a corner in the street. The Puss 'n Boots Palace was boarded up like everything else. The sign blew horizontally in the wind.

Quinn and Thorndyke exchanged glances before Thorndyke looked around. Across the street was the HARNESS LIVERY.

Thorndyke crossed to the large double doors and pounded them with his fists. After a few moments, when there had been no response, he pounded again — this time with the butt of his pistol.

Quinn pulled out his pistol and used the butt of it to hammer on the door until it was finally yanked open by a large muscular Mexican. The Mexican shook his head and started to shove the door closed when Quinn cocked his pistol and crammed it in the man's face.

The man froze with his eyes wide. Then he nodded, yes.

Quinn and Thorndyke lead their animals out of the gale and into empty stalls inside the livery.

The Mexican barred the doors closed. As the owner returned to the center of the livery, the riders emerged from the stalls carrying their weapons.

The Mexican's family, a wife and a half dozen children, all huddled around a table which was piled with food and provisions for weathering the storm.

A couple of the children were crying.

"This really a hurricane?" Thorndyke asked shouting over the sound of the wind.

"Straight from hell, Señor." The man narrowed his eyes before he said, "I will take care of your horses." To Quinn he said, "Señor, do not point a gun at me again unless you intend to kill me."

Thorndyke stepped between the Mexican and Quinn.

"Here's somethin' extra, fer your trouble." Thorndyke gave money to the Mexican. The man gave part of it back to the rancher.

"Nothing more, Señor."

Thorndyke motioned to Quinn who crossed to the side door with him. Thorndyke checked his rifle and both checked their pistols. They both even added an extra round to their side arms so as not to even leave the hammer on an empty chamber.

Thorndyke opened the door and Quinn stopped Thorndyke with a hand on his arm. He shouts in order to be heard.

"I want you to know — I heard what you were sayin'. Your story about the Comanche.

"Sometimes I talk too much."

Thorndyke stepped out into the storm and Quinn followed.

Waves from the pounding surf washed up on the street as the winds screeched. Quinn and Thorndyke fought to maintain their balance as they crossed the street toward the whore house.

Thorndyke twisted the doorbell continuously as Quinn pounded on the door frame with the butt of his pistol.

Finally the door was opened only enough to allow each man room enough to squeeze in.

Kate watched while Quinn and Thorndyke pushed past a chest of drawers which had been moved to help fortify the door. Flickering lanterns were held by Katy and Leroy, the bartender/bouncer of the house. The man was almost as big as Tarr Phillips.

The maid and some of Katy's soiled doves watched from the parlor.

Quinn and Thorndyke shook some of the water from themselves.

Katy gave the men a quick once-over and approved with a sly smile.

"You boys must be in kind of a bad way fer companionship t' fight your way through all this."

Quinn had spotted the stairs and turned to Katy.

"Is Tarr Phillips here?"

Her manner changed.

"He might be and then again he might not be."

Quinn frowned and stepped threateningly toward Katy.

Leroy saw this and started to jump Quinn when Thorndyke cracked the bouncer in the stomach with the barrel of his Winchester.

"Is he here?" Quinn demanded.

"My guess is he ain't here."

"You can guess again," Thorndyke said but Katy didn't reply.

"Then you don't mind if we check under th' beds — an' in th' garbage."

"You look wherever you're little ol' heart likes, Hun. We have lots of lookers 'round here."

Some of the girls giggled at this.

# CHAPTER 23

Quinn looked down the hall and then took the first step up the stairs. Thorndyke fell in behind. Katy casually stepped toward the secretary/desk in the hall. Thorndyke saw her move.

"Hold it!" Thorndyke said. He stepped past Katy to the secretary. He opened the lid and then pulled out a false front to a small cabinet inside. There were a series of cords, each with a small pull ring tied to it. A room number was attached to each handle.

Thorndyke set his rifle down against the side of the stairs and pulled out a Bowie knife. He leaned the desk forward slightly and then cut off all the cords at the wall behind the desk.

Thorndyke put up his knife and took up his rifle once more. He moved back behind Quinn as they started up the stairs together once more.

Quinn and Thorndyke each took a different side of the hall, stopping at each door to listen a moment. Quinn stopped at the second door on his side. He heard movement.

Quinn got ready to open the door. Thorndyke stepped forward to back him up. Quinn jerked the door open and stepped into the door, his .44 aimed.

Beyond the messed up bed, in front of a mirror which hung over a wash bowl, stood a Chinese girl.

She looked at Quinn and then at Thorndyke. She returned to her business, treating her face and body with a damp cloth. She had been severely beaten.

Quinn looked around the room and turned to the girl searching for some hint.

"Tarr Phillips," Quinn formed the words slowly.

She looked at him evenly and then motioned with her head toward the far end of the hall.

Quinn closed the door and backed into the hallway with Thorndyke. The howling of the storm continued to grow outside.

Quinn exchanged glances with Thorndyke, motioned toward the far end of the hall. They moved together.

When they arrived at the end of the hall, they took opposite sides of the door. Thorndyke reached for the knob and Quinn readied his rifle. Thorndyke twisted the knob and Quinn kicked open the door.

Tarr Phillips, dressed only in his pants and socks, turned from beside the tub as Quinn fired.

The image of Phillips shattered — it was a full length mirror reflecting the man's image.

Phillips dropped down beside the bear claw foot tub and braced himself against the side. Holding onto the tub with both hands, he kicked like a mule with both feet, slamming the door closed. Then he drew his pistol from his holster which was draped over a chair beside the tub.

He threw a couple of shots through the door as he grabbed his shotgun which leaned against the wall beside the chair. In one motion he whipped the shotgun around smashing the lamp, sending its remains pelting into the over turned tub. He ducked behind it for cover.

Quinn and Thorndyke hugged the wall on different sides of the door. Quinn chambered another two rounds in his pistol. When they were ready, Thorndyke nodded to Quinn. The farmer reached down and slowly twisted the door knob again and let the door slip open a few inches.

In the darkness Phillips waited behind the tub

his shotgun leveled at the door. When it opened and a little light from the hall streamed through the opening, he fired. The door was splintered and unhinged.

Quinn and Thorndyke were backed out of the way of Phillip's blast, which they both expected.

Thorndyke readied to dive through the door when Quinn signaled him to wait. Quinn stepped down to the door of a second bathroom beside the one Phillips occupied. Quinn opened the door and went in.

A fat aging whore had scrambled out of a soap-less tub and was reaching for a towel when Quinn rushed in. He cast only a fleeting glance at the terrified woman as he crossed to the door which connected the two baths.

He tried the knob easily. The door was locked.

Phillips was watching the splintered front door, but his eye still caught the side door knob jiggle. In an instant, Phillips finished reloading his shotgun and put two extra shells between his fingers. Then he stood and bulled his way through the wall into the hall.

Phillips burst through behind Thorndyke. The rancher barely had time to turn around before Phillips leveled his shotgun and fired.

Thorndyke was lifted off the floor and thrown down the hall dead.

# CHAPTER 24

Quinn turned around and raced to the door which led to the hall. He pulled the door open and saw Thorndyke on the floor of the hall. The door frame beside Quinn exploded.

Quinn grabbed his shoulder, dropped to the floor, throwing shots into the hall.

Bullets from Quinn's pistol splintered the wall in front of Phillips. The Ranger didn't have time to reload his scatter gun. He flung it at Quinn.

Quinn had to duck back in the bath to avoid the flying shotgun.

Phillips took a couple of running steps and dove out the covered window at the end of the hall. He shattered the glass and split the covering boards before he landed on the veranda. The storm howled into the hall.

Quinn threw more shots out the door and dove into the hall, his shoulder bleeding.

Outside the storm was now at its peak. As Phillips came crashing out the window onto the veranda, everything was in chaos. The wind was savage. It thundered and screamed. It was not like any rain known anywhere else. It was fully horizontal.

Phillips was caught by the wind which broke his fall for a moment. Then it hurled him against the side of the building and dropped him directly under the window.

He couldn't believe what he had gotten himself into. The storm made it impossible to move and impossible to hang on to anything. He tried to get his balance but that was a lost cause.

He fell and got both water and mud in his eyes. He covered his face to keep from getting hit by flying boards, branches of trees and other debris.

Back in the hall, Quinn knelt beside Thorndyke. He checked for a heartbeat but there was none. He closed the rancher's eyes.

Quinn reloaded his pistol, levered a round into the chamber of Thorndyke's rifle, and stood to go after Phillips.

Quinn stepped down to the open window, his

pistol whipping from one side to the other in search of a target. The storm came blasting through the window and directly into Quinn's face.

Phillips had toiled his way across the veranda to the railing.

Quinn was in the window behind Phillips. He fired a shot but over the roar of the storm the sound of the gunshot wasn't heard. Phillips was unaware and unaffected by Quinn's shot.

Phillips gripped the railing with all his might and slipped one leg over it. He fell and landed in the bushes below. He rolled into the flood looking up.

Quinn pulled himself through the window fighting the storm off as he went. But nothing would stop Quinn now. He made it to the railing.

Phillips fired upwards — twice at Quinn.

Quinn was not hit and climbed over the railing himself.

Phillips forced his way off through the storm and the growing flooded street.

Quinn dropped to the bushes and the mud. He got up and fought his way after Phillips.

The Ranger had made it across the open street to the harness livery. He tried to pull open the door but this was a useless effort — nothing would give. He looked over his shoulder.

Quinn was trying to follow Phillips' stumbling

in the wind and rain. There was no trail. Then Quinn thought he saw something. He looked again and could see nothing but rain.

Phillips, too, thought he saw Quinn. He tried to level his weapon and fire, but the blowing gale would not let him keep his pistol steady.

He fired a shot.

Quinn also tried to fire but had the same trouble with Thorndyke's rifle.

Quinn fired a couple of more rounds but saw no result. He pushed on.

Phillips was blown to the ground and braced himself against a water trough. With both knees drawn up and his arms tucked inside his knees, he held the pistol double handed and waited for Quinn to come.

Quinn appeared through the blowing hell for only an instant.

Phillips fired twice more and then ducked and crawled away from the trough. Phillips was blown over by the storm but he crawled on. Finally he reached a structure of some sort. It was a water tower. He took cover behind one of its large wooden beamed legs.

# CHAPTER 25

Quinn had made it to the water trough. But he had completely lost Phillips and had no idea which way to turn. Then Quinn saw the tower loom up through the storm. The next moment Quinn caught a view of Phillips. Phillips fired a braced shot from his position.

Quinn was struck in the leg, spun around by the force of the shell and then pitched off his feet by the force of the storm.

Behind the trough he got himself together. He pulled himself up and over the edge of the trough to fire at Phillips. He did get off a couple of shots, but he couldn't see what he was firing at.

Something blown by the storm, a branch of a

tree perhaps, struck Quinn and almost separated him from Thorndyke's rifle. But he hung onto it. Yet, when he checked it, the rifle was empty.

Quinn pulled his pistol and knew that Phillips was only a few feet away.

The Ranger waited for another view of Quinn to fire again.

Frustration built to a rage as Quinn fired three shots into the wind and hopefully toward Phillips.

Still Phillips waited behind the protection of the water tower's leg.

The storm was changing. Quinn looked up. The fury was dying, quickly. He added new cartridges to his pistol.

Phillips looked around, also aware that a change was occurring. He heard a deep moan from the water tower beams as it settled back from the strain of the storm.

Then the wind simply stopped. Quinn didn't understand it.

Phillips, too, was confused. The tower moaned some more, but the Ranger dismissed this, until there was a new sound — cracking timbers. Phillips looked up to see the tower collapsing on him. He screamed.

The entire structure caved in, crashing to the street.

As the tower hit the street, it dumped its

stored water. There was blue sky above. This was the calm of the storm's center.

Quinn rushed to the pile of broken wood. He holstered his pistol and tucked Thorndyke's Winchester under his arm as he began pulling off the boards one at a time in a frantic manner.

"Phillips!!! Damn you!!! Where are you!!! Phillips!!!"

He threw off boards, lifted beams and shoved them to one side as he dug down through the splintered timbers.

The side door of the livery opened and out stepped the Mexican. He looked around and up at the sky.

Other doors of other buildings opened and other people stuck their heads out.

Quinn was a madman on a mission — through the rubble.

The front door of the whore house opened and Katy and Crystal stepped out followed by Leroy and a couple of the whores.

The Mexican came up behind Quinn who continued to struggle with the unforgiving pile of wood like a man possessed.

"Señor, what are you doing?"

Quinn worked on unaware of anything but his task. Through the pile of broken boards and beams he spotted an arm. It was white as death, with a deep gash in it, blood dripping.

Quinn doubled his efforts but couldn't get past the pile of wood which had interlaced itself into a tangled knot.

The Mexican saw the arm. Thinking it was Quinn's partner the man said, "There's nothin' you can do for him, Señor."

The Mexican looked up at the sky again.

"Th' storm — she is not over."

"No!!!" shouted Quinn lost in his fight to get to Phillips. He lifted another board but couldn't pull it out. In total frustration and rage, he let out a primal scream.

"Noooooooooo!!!!!!"

The Mexican stepped up and tried to help.

Quinn went for his pistol and the Mexican reacted instantly. The shorter man pushed the weapon to one side and swung a quick and powerful right cross, flattening Quinn instantly.

The Mexican lifted Quinn as if he had no weight at all. He picked up the rifle and took it with him.

The limp, bloody arm, still visible through the debris, was left behind as the Mexican crossed toward the livery with Quinn over his shoulder. The rain began once more just as it stopped — without warning.

The wind started howling again, this time from the opposite direction. The Mexican got Quinn into the livery and pulled the door closed. Katy, Crystal, Leroy and the other girls got back inside as the hurricane returned in full fury.

※

ALL THAT REMAINED OF THE WATER TOWER AFTER the storm had passed were the broken beams which had been its legs. The storm had swept the lumber and man in it away.

Quinn sat on his horse, a bandage on his leg and one on his arm. He looked down at the clearing where he last saw what remained of Phillips.

He turned and rode away. As he went, he led Thorndyke's Appaloosa with a wrapped body draped over it.

# CHAPTER 26

The Quinn place had the look of neglect. In the early morning fog the open gate was sagging on its hinges but wild grass and weeds grew in the yard.

A very weary Lyles Quinn rode into the yard, still leading Thorndyke's horse. The barrel of a shotgun appeared from behind the now empty wagon near the barn. The double barrels followed the rider's every movement.

Quinn pulled up in front of the farmhouse. He was in pain from both his wounds.

The voice from behind the shotgun called out, "Hold up there!"

Quinn stopped and turned slowly letting his hand casually move toward his pistol as he pivoted in the saddle.

"Touch that gun butt an' it'll be th' last thing you ever touch."

Quinn relaxed his hand and strained to see who was speaking from across the yard.

"A man doesn't like to be threatened on his own land."

"Quinn?"

The shotgun was lowered and Luther Bobbs, the stage coach wrangler stepped from behind the wagon, the weapon still in his hands.

"Didn't rec'nize ya'. My eyes ain't what they used t' be."

"Mr. Bobbs?"

"Yup."

"What are you doing out here?"

"Your job. Th' St. Clair's pulled out a week ago. The rest are all leavin', too."

Quinn quickly looked toward the house, a look of panic on his face.

"She's all right. I seen t' that," Bobbs said.

"Thanks."

"Didn't do it fer you."

Bobbs glanced toward the house.

"She's a good woman. If'n she was mine, I wouldn't leave her alone -- on no account."

Quinn knew Bobbs was right.

He eased his injured leg across his saddle and

dismounted tying his horse to the hitching post. Then he started to limp up towards the house.

Bobbs crossed to the other horse where the body was tied across the saddle.

"Ya' get 'im? Th' one that —"

Bobbs didn't know how to put it into words. Quinn shook his head.

"It's Zeak Thorndyke. He wanted to be buried on his own land. Next to his wife and son. It was the least I could do."

"Don't see how it'd make much difference now."

"It was important to him."

Bobbs sighed.

"Why don't ya' let me see t' Zeak. He was m' friend."

"I'd like to think he was mine, too."

"Quinn, you got a wife in there that needs ya'. Zeak don't no more. You done your part. You brung him back. I'll finish it."

Quinn considered this idea and then agreed with a nod of his head.

"Why don't you keep th' horse and saddle?" he said to Bobbs.

Bobbs said, "I could do that."

Bobbs stepped up to Thorndyke's horse and saw the Winchester in the saddle scabbard. He pulled it out.

"You probably ought t' keep this." Bobbs carried the rifle to Quinn. Quinn accepted the rifle without a word. Quinn turned to the door and tried the knob. It was locked. He knocked but heard nothing.

"Sarah?"

No response but there was a sound of wood on wood from inside. Suddenly Quinn sensed something was wrong. He tried the door again and this time forced it open. Quinn hobbled in.

He discovered Sarah hanging at the end of a rope which has been thrown over the main support beam in the center of the farmhouse. A chair, on its side, only a few feet away.

Horrified, Quinn dropped the rifle and rushed to her. He lifted his wife's limp form by the legs, taking the weight off the rope.

Suddenly Luther Bobbs was there beside him, a knife in his hand. Bobbs sliced the rope and Sarah dropped into Quinn's arms.

Sarah's face was blue, the knot around her neck badly tied but tight. Quinn freed it. He held her, but she was not breathing. He didn't know what to do.

Quinn looked up at Bobbs who was also at a loss.

Then, after an eternal moment Sarah's body convulsed and she gasped for air. Tears came to

Quinn's eyes as his unspoken prayer was answered.

She gasped for other breaths until she was breathing regularly again.

"She must'a heard us outside. And it scared her," Quinn said.

Her eyes opened as he clutched her body to his, rocking her in his arms as if she were a child. Then her arms went around his neck and she clung to him.

"Sarah! Sarah! Sarah!"

# CHAPTER 27

Quinn sat on the front porch bench, his shirt off. Sarah was beside him with a stack of clean rags and a pan of water. She had a bandage around her throat. She was working on his shoulder wound.

Sarah dabbed at it carefully. He flinched.

"I'm sorry," she said.

"It's all right," he assured her.

The sweat poured off his forehead. His injuries hurt more than he was letting on.

"How are you doing?" he asked her through gritted teeth.

"Why don't we leave this open for a while? You sit here and let it get some fresh air."

"All right."

"But I do want to put that arm in a sling before we're finished. As long as you keep moving it —"

"I know."

"How's your leg?"

"It'll keep for a while."

She looked down at him as she stood. She realized that this was his way of saying that he was still in pain but would deal with it himself for the moment. She nodded.

"But the first thing after supper — "

She leaned over and gave him a hesitant but definite kiss. She then took the bandages into the house.

Quinn watched her go trying to understand the change. She came back and stood beside him.

"Now, you rest a while."

"I could clean Thorndyke's rifle. It's just inside the door," he pointed.

"It'll wait, too," she said.

He sat back as Sarah went down the steps to the yard.

As she looked around the farm, Sara thrust her hands into the pockets of her dress. She pulled out the carved wooden horse Luther Bobbs had given her. She looked at it a moment and smiled.

She slipped it back in her pocket, stepped around to the side of the house where she picked up a sickle. She began to chop the grass away from the porch.

After she had cleared a space, she puts the implement on the edge of the porch and got a hoe. A few plants from before had survived. Sarah began to turn over the dirt to make room for the survivors to grow.

TWO RIDERS PULLED TO A HALT ON A HILL WHERE the Quinn place could be seen in the distance. One of the two riders was Texas Ranger Captain Billy Luke.

"I'll call him out. I want to have some talkin' before there's any shootin'."

He looked at the other rider.

"An' I don't want this farmer killed less'n we have 't. You hear me?"

The other rider was Tarr Phillips — bandaged, scarred and bruised but very much alive.

"That bastard tried t' kill a Texas Ranger."

"Accordin' to what I've learned, he had cause."

Captain Luke took out his pistol and checked it before he returned it to his holster.

"Still, let's let not take any chances."

Phillips also slipped his pistol from its holster. In a quick move he swung his gun hand out, catching Captain Luke across the side of the head and knocking the old ranger out of the saddle.

Captain Luke hit the ground and didn't move.

Phillips holstered his pistol and then moved off in a flanking move around the farm house.

SWEATING FROM HER LABORS ON THE FLOWER bed/garden, Sarah went to the rain barrel at the back corner of the house. Here she got a bucket full of the cool, clear water and returned to her freshly planted rows.

She poured water on the plants, one at a time. Even though most were wilted and some almost assuredly dead, a couple appeared to have at least a prayer of reviving and perhaps even thriving.

She made a second trip to the rain barrel and was watering again when the shadow of Phillips came up behind her. He grabbed her and she dropped the bucket to the ground.

Phillips had Sarah with a hand over her mouth, a rifle in his other hand. Phillips twisted her around toward the front porch where Quinn had dozed off. He awoke to the muffled sounds of his wife's struggle.

It registered that Sarah was in danger and Tarr Phillips was still alive. He heaved himself up, only to slump half way up from the pain of his injured leg.

Seeing that Quinn was no immediate threat, Phillips smiled and released Sarah enough to swing her around so she could see him. She froze when she saw who it was.

"Told you not t' make nothin' out of it." He looked up at Quinn. "Now, I'm goin have t' kill him."

"Noooo!!!" she screamed.

Phillips laughed and said, "An' when I'm through w'th him, I got somethin' in mind fer you."

She shrank back.

Quinn forced himself to move across the porch. He stopped at the top step.

"Come on down," Phillips taunted.

Quinn gathered his strength.

"No, Lyles!" Sarah yelled.

Quinn started down the steps, bracing himself on the porch beam.

Phillips threw Sarah aside and she fell in the dirt. Phillips stepped toward Quinn.

Quinn was sweating profusely and breathing hard as he came face to face with Phillips.

"Next time, plow-boy, if there ever was goin t' be a next time, you best make sure you've kilt me."

Quinn tried to steady himself. "You going to let

me at least have a gun?" he asked looking at Phillips' rifle.

"You must be loco. This ain't goin' t' be no fair fight. I'm goin'a kill you, boy. That's all there is to it."

Quinn took a breath. He was not afraid. He lunged at Phillips.

# CHAPTER 28

Phillips stepped aside easily and Quinn landed in the dirt.

Sarah was a mass of tears and terror as she watched.

Quinn got up, the dirt all over his shoulder wounds, the blood coming more freely and making a bloody mud pack. He was in a more pain than he had ever known. Still he managed to get himself up again. His breath came in heavy gasps when he finally regained his feet.

Phillips used his rifle barrel as a poker and jabbed Quinn's shoulder injuries.

"Looks like I got you a couple of times in that storm."

Quinn flinched in pain, staggered back, favoring his injured leg.

"How's that leg doin'?"

Phillips poked Quinn in the thigh, the farmer tried to grab the rifle, but Phillips was too quick. Quinn moved back.

Sarah was almost at the edge of her sanity. She stood and tried to flee but she stumbled and went down again.

Phillips glanced back at Sarah but didn't pay much attention to her. He was intent on Quinn. With a cruel smile he stepped forward and butt stroked Quinn's injured leg with his rifle.

An audible crack of bone was heard as Quinn yelled and dropped to the ground unconscious.

Sarah eyes were wide with terror. She screamed. "No! ! ! ! ! !"

Phillips stepped over to where Quinn lay. He jabbed the farmer in his injuries. Quinn jerked with pain.

"Ahaaaaaa! ! ! ! !" he yelled coming to.

"Come on, Hoss. You wasn't 'round last time. I want you t' watch this time."

Suddenly Sarah was behind Phillips, the sickle raised above her head. She gathered all of her strength for an instant before she brought the weapon down with all her strength. She buried its blade as deep as she could in Phillips' back.

Phillips stiffened and groaned from the blow and dropped his rifle. But he didn't fall.

He turned, the implement protruding from his back, and advanced on the stunned Sarah. She tried to back away but she had been so overcome with terror that her feet did not respond to her brain.

Suddenly Phillips was on her and crushed her against the porch with his weight. He held her there trying to reach the weapon in his back.

Quinn dragged himself up the steps.

There was a gurgling sound to Phillips labored breathing, as if blood were collecting in one of his lungs. He held on to the woman with both hands.

He reached for her hair with one hand while going for his knife with the other. He brought the blade up to the widow's peak of her forehead.

"You goin t' be a long time dying."

Phillips started to pull the blade across her head. But before he could, the Ranger jerked and froze as two rifle shots rang out. Phillips fell to the ground.

Captain Billy Luke, a rifle in his hands, leaned over the outer most fence of the Quinn farm.

Sarah had blood now in her eyes from the small cut Phillips made with his blade. But she brushed it away as she ran to where Quinn lay in the doorway, Thorndyke's smoking rifle in his hands.

Billy Luke walked into the yard leading his horse. He crossed over to the body of Tarr Phillips. The evil Ranger's dead eyes were open to the sun.

"Like I told you — this was ranger business," Billy Luke said.

❦

QUINN SAT ON THE WAGON SEAT. HE HAD ONE arm in a sling and his injured leg splinted and propped up on the front lip of the wagon.

Captain Billy Luke carried a chair from the house to the wagon where he loaded it with the other household furnishings. He looked over at Sarah.

Sarah was on her knees in the garden picking some seeds out of the dirt.

Luke looked up at Quinn. The Ranger nodded toward the house.

"Sure about th' bed?"

"Leave it."

"And th' -- rest?"

"Burn it. It's a good house. Maybe somebody can have a good life here. Fire burns clean. They can build on the foundation."

"You could do that."

Sarah walked up to the wagon, a bandage around her head.

"We have to find another place. Maybe Colorado."

Captain Luke took a lantern out of the wagon to the porch and poured the kerosene out onto the floor and into the house. Then he struck a match and tossed it into the living room before he returned to the wagon. He put the lantern in the back.

Sarah saw something behind the wagon. She stooped and picked up several carved wooden horses on the ground among a mass of wood shavings.

Sarah showed the new carved horses to Quinn. She smiled.

Quinn smiled as Captain Luke helped her onto the wagon seat.

Luke climbed onto his horse. The Ranger Captain picked up the bridle of Phillips's horse. Phillips's body was wrapped and tied over the second horse.

"Where are you taking him?" Quinn asked.

The older Ranger looked out toward the prairie. "Somewhere out there. I'll dig him a hole but I won't leave a marker." He looked down and spat. "I'm sorry fer what he did. Wish there was somethin' else I could do or say. There just ain't."

Captain Luke rode out of the farm yard.

The Quinns rode out in the opposite direction.

JACK R. STANLEY

The house with its hauntings burned fiercely and the smoke smeared across the Texas sky.

## THE END

# THANK YOU

Thank you for taking the time to read <u>Occurrence At Latigo</u>. I hope you enjoyed it. If you did, please consider posting a short review on line at the site where you purchased the book and telling your friends. Word of mouth is an author's best friend and much appreciated. I love to write these stories, but it's even better to sell some and to know other people take some joy from them, too.

If you're interested is subscribing to my monthly newsletter, contact me at jacks@wright-bridgepress.com. You know when my next novel is coming out and a little bit about how I work. I would love to hear from you.

THANK YOU

Thank you,
   Jack R. Stanley

# TWO FREE E-BOOKS

## *[Murder in Muleshoe]*
**If you were murdered would they try to find the killer or plan him a parade?**

## *[Guns Along The Rio]Rio*
**In 1858, two fresh-off-the-ranch 17-year-olds join the Texas Rangers. What could possibly go wrong?**

Click HERE to get your free books.

# ABOUT THE AUTHOR

Jack R. Stanley is an award winning novelist, play-wright, and screenwriter. As an officer and combat photographer in Vietnam, he earned the Bronze Star. Yet he says, "When you're in a firefight and everybody else on both side have guns while you have a camera --- you get to change your pants a lot."

After his military service he received both his M.A. and his Ph.D. at the University of Michigan in Ann Arbor in Radio-TV-Film. His doctoral dissertation was on the long running TV series GUN-SMOKE. Stanley also received two of Michigan's most prestigious creative writing awards, The Hopwood Award, one for a one-act play and the second for a novel.

Still married to his gifted high school sweet-heart, Stanley's first academic position was TV Area Head at The University of Texas at Austin's Department of Radio-TV-Film. He later moved to deep-south Texas and the Lower Rio Grande

Valley for a challenging position with The University of Texas-Pan American. Here he taught Theatre-TV-Film for 30 years in the Department of Communication serving as Department Chair at U.T.P.A. for 11 years. He did take one year out to work for The University of Alaska Anchorage as a visiting professor. Back in Texas, Stanley directed for stage at The University Theatre, produced and directed fifteen student staffed, cast, and crewed feature films, writing most of the original screenplays. Just a few of his credits are available on IMDB.com.

He now lives in the Texas Panhandle where he writes his fiction.

Through A Lens Darkly: Vietnam

[Mysteries]

Murder In Muleshoe

Corpse In Canyon

The Lovecraft Murders

*Short Stories*

TALES FROM THE ALASKAN GOLD RUSH

Klondike Justice

Dangerous Camp On The Kenai

The Winds of Skagway

*Screenplays*

6 and 10

The 7$^{th}$ Luger

Afternoon Delight

Angel's Revenge

Between Love And Murder

Blood Drive

Death Scene

The Defection of Grigori Dorsky

The Evil Eye

Fatty and Hearst

Gideon: The Horse That Saved Texas

Hell In Paradise

Hollowpoint

Holiday For An Assassin

Horse Thief Hollow

Incident A tLajitas

Love, Lust, & Life

Mom & Apple Pye

Pancho's Pilot

The Prometheus Peril

The Rape of Sarah Quinn

Reservations

River of Tears

Seven Reasons Why

The Thing About Love

The Texas Rattlesnake Murders

Too Good To Be True

The Vampire Rose

A Violent End

The Virgin Casanova

*Plays*

Antigone In Texas

Cyrano

The Last Virgin From Las Vegas

The Seven Keys

The Unwed Widow

www.ingramcontent.com/pod-product-compliance
Lightning Source LLC
Chambersburg PA
CBHW032016170626

46807CB00006B/2837